"My mo͟ club."

Why had that come out of his mouth? "They only read romance novels."

There. He'd warned her.

"How kind of her." She glanced away. "It's not a good time. I'll have to pass."

Disappointment warred with relief. "I don't blame you. Not much of a reader myself."

"I like to read."

"Not romance novels, though."

"I like romance novels."

"Oh."

"It's not the books. I'd be embarrassed if I fainted there. And I have Peanut. He's big. I wouldn't want it to be awkward."

"You clearly don't know my mom. No dog is too big for her house. No amount of fainting would deter her."

He couldn't remember the last time he'd gone to anyone's house other than Cade's or his mother's. Yet he felt comfortable at Ashlinn's. She was easy to be with, fun to talk to, and he was glad they were planning the event together. Should he start taking advantage of what Jewel River had to offer?

Maybe if Ashlinn was by his side.

Jill Kemerer is a *Publishers Weekly* bestselling author of heartwarming, emotional, small-town romance novels often featuring cowboys. Over three-quarters of a million of her books have sold worldwide. Jill's essentials include coffee, caramels, a stack of books and long walks outdoors. She resides in Ohio with her husband, and they have two adult children. Jill loves connecting with readers. Please visit her website, jillkemerer.com, or contact her at PO Box 2802, Whitehouse, OH 43571.

Books by Jill Kemerer

Love Inspired

Wyoming Legacies

The Cowboy's Christmas Compromise
United by the Twins
Training the K-9 Companion
The Cowboy's Christmas Treasures
The Cowboy's Easter Surprise
His New Companion

Wyoming Ranchers

The Prodigal's Holiday Hope
A Cowboy to Rely On
Guarding His Secret
The Mistletoe Favor
Depending on the Cowboy
The Cowboy's Little Secret

Visit the Author Profile page at LoveInspired.com for more titles.

HIS NEW COMPANION

JILL KEMERER

LOVE INSPIRED
INSPIRATIONAL ROMANCE

LOVE INSPIRED®
INSPIRATIONAL ROMANCE

Recycling programs
for this product may
not exist in your area.

ISBN-13: 978-1-335-93732-2

His New Companion

Copyright © 2025 by Ripple Effect Press, LLC

Love Inspired
22 Adelaide St. West, 41st Floor
Toronto, Ontario M5H 4E3, Canada
www.LoveInspired.com

Printed in Lithuania

MIX
Paper | Supporting
responsible forestry
FSC® C021394

For I reckon that the sufferings of this present time
are not worthy to be compared with
the glory which shall be revealed in us.
—*Romans* 8:18

To Melissa Endlich, Shana Asaro, Tina James and Rachel Kent. The Wyoming Legacies series wouldn't have been published without you. Thank you for believing in my books and giving me the opportunity to write them.

To Sophie and Harvey, the inspiration for Peanut and Fritz. Our late black-and-tan miniature dachshund and my sister's golden retriever always got along like peanut butter and jelly. Sophie, you'll forever be in my heart.

Chapter One

He would *not* get attached to the dog. After all, this was a temporary gig.

Ty Moulten stood outside the entrance of Howard Service Dogs in Jewel River, Wyoming, after five on Friday and wondered again if fostering a dog on the weekends was wise. Maybe he should wait until next year when he'd have more time to get used to the idea. Or he could try in a few months when the temperature cooled. July had been a scorcher so far, and they were only midway through it.

Either the sun was melting him or he'd worked himself into an actual fever. Why was he so sweaty? Probably didn't help that after he'd finished checking cattle, he'd opted to change into a fresh pair of jeans instead of shorts.

Life made more sense in jeans, cowboy boots and a cowboy hat. And being comfortable would help him keep his head on straight. His heart had been broken once. Shattered, really. Fostering a dog was nothing compared to what he'd had with Zoey, but it didn't change the fact there wasn't enough of his heart left for him to squander the little that remained.

He didn't do love—or people in general—anymore.

Ty opened the glass door, stepped into the small entryway and continued through a second set of glass doors. Inside the warehouse, industrial-sized fans overhead circulated the air, and the large space in front of him had been sectioned into training areas. To the far left, a door led to the kennel room, and to the far right stood the office and a hallway leading to restrooms and storage.

Patrick Howard had moved to Jewel River after purchasing the abandoned warehouse from Ty's older brother, Cade. Patrick's daughter, Mackenzie, had opened her veterinary clinic in the smaller building next door. Their arrival had worked out great for the community as well as for the Moulten family. The area had a veterinarian again, and Mackenzie and Cade had gotten married in January. The training center's renovations had taken the better part of last year.

Ty's mother, Christy Moulten, had been the one to convince Ty to volunteer there. For someone who'd spent the past six years on his ranch avoiding extended interaction with anyone besides his brother and mom, the idea had sounded ludicrous. But then it had grown on him. Helping Patrick meant helping people who needed a service dog. Fostering a dog on weekends for a cause he believed in? Yeah, he could probably handle that.

"You made it." Patrick emerged from his office with his German shepherd, Charger, by his side. The tall, lean man in his early sixties wore athletic shorts, a T-shirt and running shoes. He strode toward Ty. "I appreciate you doing this for me. Hope you don't mind, but there's been a slight change in plans."

Ty didn't like the sound of that. He braced himself as Patrick stopped a few feet in front of him.

"I'm worried about Fritz."

"Who's Fritz?" Ty asked.

"I'll show you." Patrick jerked his thumb toward the kennels. "Let's go."

Ty followed him to the large kennel room. Shuffling noises, whining and a few barks greeted them. Patrick stopped near a crate that contained a black-and-tan miniature dachshund.

"Fritz is three years old. I brought him here last week. His owner, a retired veteran, passed away, and the family couldn't keep the dog. A dachshund rescuer told me this guy was trained to help his owner with anxiety and depression. Naturally, I hoped to work with him and place him with one of my clients."

"You don't think you'll be able to?" Ty peered down to get a glimpse of the dog, but he was curled up in the rear corner.

"I'm not sure. At this point, no. He's miserable here even when he's out with the other dogs. I think he was attached to his owner and needs one-on-one attention."

Ty could see where this was headed, and panic zipped through him. He'd expected to get a bigger, easygoing dog that didn't need much attention. He'd pictured the two of them walking around his ranch or hanging out in his living room from Friday night through Monday morning.

"Hey, Fritz, come on out." Patrick bent and opened the kennel door. The dog slowly emerged, stretching his legs in front of him. Then he shook his body—ears flapping loudly—and trotted directly to Ty.

Those big brown eyes melted him. Fritz's tail wagged as he sniffed Ty's shoes. Then he began wiggling ecstatically with what appeared to be a smile on his face.

"Well, I'll be." Patrick rubbed his chin. "I haven't seen him this excited since bringing him here. He likes you."

Ty crouched and let the dog sniff the back of his hand before attempting to pet him. Fritz ate up the attention. He was wiggling so much that Ty laughed and picked him up. The dog instantly settled in his arms.

"Would you be willing to take Fritz for the weekend?" Patrick asked.

As if on cue, Fritz turned to stare up at him with eyes full of longing. Stirrings in his heart threw him off balance. This dog liked him. Really liked him. And he couldn't weigh ten pounds. The warm little body with his soft, short fur was evaporating all the arguments warring in Ty's brain.

He promptly set the dog down and rocked back on his heels.

"What would it entail?" Ty had already filled out the necessary paperwork to volunteer. He'd watched the video on understanding a dog's body language. Reviewed training techniques with Patrick and with his mother, who'd trained her Pomeranian, Tulip, to be a therapy dog. But he'd mentally prepared himself to take care of a large dog, not this bitty thing.

"Doxies are energetic, vocal, loving dogs." Patrick picked up Fritz and stroked his back. The dog stared mournfully at Ty. "They're quick learners, always on alert. He'll enjoy being around the horses. Expect him to follow you around all the time. He'll want to be on your lap whenever you're sitting. Fritz is well trained. He'll sleep in a crate. But he'll be your shadow during the day."

Ty liked the idea of having a buddy, but this dog with its take-me-home eyes worried him. How could he avoid getting attached?

"What will happen to him if I don't take him for the weekend?"

Patrick waved as if not to worry. "I've got volunteers coming in tomorrow and Sunday. He'll be taken care of."

That meant the dog would be as gloomy as he was before Ty arrived.

"What dog were you originally going to have me take this weekend?" He eyed the line of kennels.

"Nico." Patrick backed up three steps to a chocolate Lab's kennel. "He's only got three more weeks here, and he'll be off to his new home."

Nico was grooming his paw. The dog looked pretty chill. Fritz, on the other hand, was wriggling to get out of Patrick's arms. The man set him down, and he zoomed to Ty's feet and let out a yip. Then he sat up on his hind legs with his paws in the air.

Ty couldn't ignore that demonstration. Who could? Anticipation built, and he picked up the dog again. Fritz heaved a sigh of contentment.

"Like I said, this is the first I've seen him show any excitement, and I've had him for over a week. Proves my point. He lost his human, and I don't think he'll thrive here, let alone with a client, if I don't do something to help him."

"What's going to happen to him come Monday?" He'd liked the feel of the dog in his arms too much.

"Maybe a weekend with you will snap him out of it. If not, I'll find him a home. A formally trained, well-behaved miniature dachshund like this will be in high demand."

"If you think Fritz would be better off with me this weekend, I guess I can take him."

"It would give me peace of mind, especially seeing how he feels about you. I'm going to be out of town most of the weekend, and I don't like thinking of him all dumpy and depressed here."

"I'll do it." Two minutes. That was all it had taken for him to want this dog. He was already growing too attached.

Maybe this was a bad idea.

Why was he worrying? Patrick would find Fritz a home,

and Ty would forget about him. He'd go on to foster other dogs, bigger dogs.

"I really appreciate it. Let's go to my office." Patrick led the way. Ty carried Fritz. Man, he was cute. His ears and tail were black like the rest of his body. Tan eyebrows and long eyelashes topped his expressive brown eyes. The fur on his paws and neck was tan, too. He seemed right at home in Ty's arms. Ty was so taken with the mutt he didn't even realize someone else was in the office until he walked in.

"Ashlinn!" Patrick beamed as he hugged the woman wearing a sundress and slip-on canvas sneakers.

She had long blond hair and big blue eyes. She was thin— very thin—and pretty—very pretty. A golden retriever wearing a service-dog vest sat by her side. She held the handle of the dog's harness. Was it *her* service dog? Or one in training?

"I figured I'd stop by before you locked up for the night." Her soft voice strained as if it took effort to speak.

"Are you all settled in?" Patrick gestured for her to sit, and she lowered herself into the chair.

"I'm getting there. Mom and Dad finished unpacking the kitchen. Everything else is pretty much done. They're driving back on Sunday."

"I'm glad it's working out." Patrick remained standing. "Ashlinn, this is Ty Moulten. He's one of our volunteers fostering dogs on weekends." Patrick addressed Ty. "Ty, this is my new assistant, Ashlinn Burnier. She'll be dealing with the administrative tasks around here from time to time."

"Nice to meet you." He nodded, still holding the dog.

She gave him a shy smile. "You, too."

Patrick addressed Ashlinn again. "Let me get everything for Ty to take Fritz, and then you and I can talk. Just sit tight."

She patted the head of the dog sitting next to her. "No worries. I've got Peanut."

"I'll be giving him a warm welcome, too, in a minute." Patrick went over to a stack of supplies in the corner. "All right, Ty, here's his crate. Easy to put together—like this." He gave a quick demonstration, and it did look simple to assemble. "This bin has his food, treats, toys and harness. Here, I'll show you how to put it on."

Patrick demonstrated how to put on the harness, clipped the leash to it and handed the leash to Ty. Then he explained how the booster seat would work in his truck.

"Anything else I need to know?" Ty asked, holding the leash. Fritz had sniffed his way toward Peanut, but they remained a few feet apart. With his mouth slightly open and tongue panting, Peanut watched the small dog.

"I can't think of anything. Text or call me with any questions or concerns. Mackenzie's always available, too, and I know you have her number." Patrick motioned for the two of them to leave the office. He picked up the crate, while Ty hefted the bag with supplies.

"It was nice to meet you," Ashlinn said.

"You, too. Um, welcome to Jewel River." He didn't mean to stare, but the smile on her face reminded him of last week's fireworks. Dazzling.

"Thanks."

He gave her a nod, then hurried out of there with Fritz trotting next to him. Once they'd loaded everything in his truck and gotten the harness clipped to Fritz's booster seat in the passenger side, Ty waved goodbye to Patrick and drove away.

The dog sat in the doggy seat with his front paws on the top, and he panted eagerly as the truck gained speed.

"You like driving around, huh? I do, too."

A sense of excitement—of actually looking forward to something for once—overcame him. Then, right on cue, anxiety flared. He liked this dog. But it wasn't his. Patrick would find it a home soon, so he'd better not get used to having it around.

His thoughts turned to Ashlinn. The dog wearing the vest must be hers. And that meant…

The beautiful woman needed a service dog. And if she needed one, there was a reason for it. A medical reason.

A lifetime ago, he'd fallen in love with Zoey Daniels, knowing she had cystic fibrosis. He'd asked her to marry him, and she'd accepted. Less than two months before their wedding, she'd died from complications due to the disease.

He had no regrets. He'd do it all again—fall in love with the vibrant girl with long brown hair, freckles on her nose and hazel eyes. He'd known she'd probably die young, but neither of them had thought it would be so soon.

He counted himself blessed to have loved her. But there could only ever be one Zoey. And he couldn't—wouldn't—go through a loss like that again.

She'd died six years ago, and time hadn't healed his wounds. He'd learned to live with them, and that was about all he could hope for. His dream of having a wife had been buried with Zoey. There would be no other woman in his life.

Ashlinn kept her breathing steady while Patrick helped Ty. Peanut sat on his haunches next to her. The fact he was relaxed boded well. She'd had two fainting spells since arriving last night. Her mother had fussed, and her father had declared moving here was a mistake and they should return to South Dakota where they could keep an eye on her.

Her parents worried about her. With good reason.

But she wasn't moving back to South Dakota. She wasn't moving back in with them, either. Her disease had made her ill for six years, four of which she'd been mostly bedridden in her childhood home. Last year, with the help of various treatments and getting Peanut, her medical alert dog, she'd slowly been able to have something that resembled a life.

When Patrick had offered her this job, the prospect had been a bright light in a murky future. She'd be able to walk to work—a necessity since she might never be able to drive. She could use the business skills she'd learned in college. And best of all, Patrick could train dogs to recognize a variety of symptoms simply by being around her. Other people dealing with blood pressure problems, migraines and fatigue would benefit from the dogs she'd be interacting with at the center.

She couldn't think of a better job if she tried. It wasn't like she could work anywhere else, either. Between the syncope—fainting episodes—and her stomach problems, it was unlikely she'd ever be able to work full-time again. With the help of her parents and medical team, she'd applied and qualified for disability benefits to help pay her living expenses.

"Sorry about that. Now, where were we?" Patrick came back into the office and took a seat behind the desk. "How's the house? Will it suit your needs?"

"It's perfect." Ashlinn adored the two-bedroom, one-story home built in the 1950s only a block away from the training center. The rooms had been freshly painted before she signed the lease, and it had a fenced-in backyard for Peanut.

"Your folks coming around to the idea of you living here, yet?"

"No." She shook her head, suppressing a grimace. "Every five minutes they remind me I can change my mind at any time and drive back with them. I'm trying to be patient, but I had to get out of there."

"This is hard for them, too." Patrick had a gift for understanding the challenges people like her faced.

"I know." The guilt she'd been grappling with eased slightly. "I appreciate them and all they've done for me."

"I know you do. How have you been holding up? Physically?" His concern reminded her she had someone in her corner here. She wouldn't be alone. Well, she'd mostly be alone, but she had Patrick and Mackenzie looking out for her, and that counted for a lot.

"Decent. As soon as we arrived, I set up a couple of stations for when I pass out. One in the living room and one in the bedroom. Peanut approves."

"Glad to hear it. What are you using for the stations?"

"Weighted blankets, a few pillows. I have an ottoman to elevate my legs if need be."

"Have you had to use them?"

"Yes." She petted the dog. "It was just like at home. This guy licked me and went straight to the blanket in the living room. I chugged some water, got on the floor and had him sit to cover my legs. I wasn't out long. Mom said he stayed right by my side and nudged and nibbled my arm until I recovered. I think she's been worried that the move will affect Peanut's ability to alert me."

"I guess he passed that test with flying colors."

"Exactly."

"Keep in mind, I'm only a minute away if you need anything."

"Thanks. I appreciate it. I think I'll be okay. I talked to the manager of the supermarket, and they'll deliver my groceries once a week. The man mentioned a few retirees who can drive me places if I need a ride somewhere." She didn't anticipate going anywhere besides work. Too risky. And embarrassing. She couldn't bear the thought of passing out in front of people, and she tended to pass out a few times each day.

"Peanut is legally allowed to go most places with you. Don't forget that." Patrick had his stern face on. "According to the ADA, you qualify as disabled. The effects of your autoimmune disease have been debilitating, and if anyone questions you bringing Peanut into church or a store, you can tell them to talk to me. I'll set them straight."

While it was nice of him to offer, she had no plans to get out much. Having her own house and a limited part-time job would be taxing enough.

"You said your folks are heading back on Sunday?" he asked.

She nodded. "I'll come in on Monday."

"Your schedule is entirely up to you. If you can only work for an hour once or twice a week, that's fine. I don't want you overexerting yourself."

"You sound like my dad." She smiled. She and Patrick had discussed appropriate working hours at length. They'd agreed she'd come in for an hour or two on weekdays—but only if she felt up to it. If she didn't, she'd stay home. "Don't worry. I'll listen to my body. Peanut's great at letting me know when my blood pressure's dropping. And I'll play it by ear for a while. Give it a few weeks. I should be settled by then."

They talked for a while longer and said their goodbyes. Outside, the sunshine and slight breeze were such welcome sensations on her skin, she couldn't help raising her face to the sky. *God, You've blessed me with improved health, a dog that knows my body better than I do, a house of my own and a job tailor-made for me. Please bless this new phase in my life.*

"Come on, Peanut. We're going on patrol." They headed across the parking lot. For years, she'd barely been able to go outside, and she certainly hadn't been able to enjoy it when she did. And here she was. Independent-ish. At last.

Peanut walked in a heel beside her, and her thoughts strayed to Ty. What a handsome cowboy. She wasn't sure what to make of him. He seemed quiet. He'd cradled the little dog like he would a baby—protective and gentle.

A pang pinched her heart. No babies for her. No husband or boyfriend, either. Her life had veered off course during her sophomore year of college. As a twenty-year-old, she'd started getting bouts of severe stomach cramping. Then blood in her stools. Occasionally, she'd vomit for no apparent reason. After the doctors had run all their tests and told her stress was causing her health problems, she'd pushed herself to finish the semester. Then, on top of the other health issues, the fainting had started during her junior year of college, and her life had launched off a cliff.

Those had been dark days. Ashlinn tried not to think about them. They were too depressing.

As pleased as she was to move to Jewel River, this wasn't what she'd thought her life would look like at twenty-six. Yes, it would be wonderful to dream about a future with a gorgeous cowboy and a few babies, but that was all it would ever be—a fantasy.

At the stop sign, she checked for traffic, then continued forward with Peanut next to her. There was no use thinking about what she didn't have—what she'd never have. She'd focus on her blessings, instead. She had plenty of those.

A slice of independence. A purpose in life. The best dog in the world. Parents who loved her…a little too much.

Two houses ahead, her mom stood on the front porch and waved. Ashlinn waved back. In no time, she and Peanut had joined her.

"How did it go?" Mom took her arm to lead her inside. Ashlinn tactfully slid it free.

"It went well."

Her mother grabbed for her hand, and this time she yanked it away.

"I'm okay, Mom. You don't need to help me. I'm fine on my own."

Her mother's eyes narrowed as she sighed. "This move is taking a lot out of you. Moving takes a lot out of everyone. I don't want you to fall and crack your head open."

"Peanut would be licking my hand or nudging me if my blood pressure was dipping."

"I know." She shut the door once they were inside. "But I still think you need to be careful."

Ashlinn bent to take off Peanut's service-dog vest. "Good boy. You were awesome out there." She petted his head and scratched behind his ears. As soon as she was done, the dog took off to the kitchen, where her dad praised him. Was probably showering him with treats, too.

"The poor dog is going to miss you guys." Ashlinn sat on the couch and let her head fall back against the cushions. "He didn't know how good he had it living with you."

"We'll miss you both. It's going to be an adjustment for all of us." Her mother's brave face looked dangerously close to cracking. "I hate leaving you here alone. Are you sure this is what you want?"

Irritation grew, but she tamped it down. What had Patrick said? To be patient with them. He was right. They'd done so much for her—putting their lives on hold for years to take care of her—and the least she could do was try to reassure them about her decision to move here.

"I'm sure." She nodded. "This is more than I'd hoped for. Patrick understands my limitations. I don't have to worry about the fact I can't get a driver's license. And there's a medical clinic less than a mile away."

"But…you'll be alone. What if you fall and hurt yourself? Peanut can't call 911 for help."

"Patrick and his daughter are going to check on me, and if they can't, one of their friends will. They'll both have keys to get in if there's an emergency." Her mom's concerns had been at the top of her list, too, and she'd forever be grateful for Patrick and Mackenzie for offering to help her.

"What if your symptoms get worse? This could be a temporary reprieve."

The doctors weren't sure why her symptoms had improved so drastically over the past couple of years. They'd experimented with numerous treatments, including several sessions of plasmapheresis—a total plasma exchange—which should have only produced short-term results. The treatments had allowed her to stand without passing out, and she'd no longer been bedridden. For reasons no one could explain, she'd continued to improve without additional plasmapheresis sessions. She'd slowly gained strength, and her dad had contacted a company about getting a medical alert dog. Patrick had been the trainer. He'd paired her with Peanut. Her life had improved a million-fold in just a year's time since getting him.

"You're right. My good health might be temporary. And if it is, you'll be the first to know."

Her mother came over and sat next to her, taking her hand in hers. "You'll always have a home with us. You're never a burden. We love you, and if there's any reason at all you need us to come get you, we will."

Tears pricked her eyes. She didn't deserve this kind of love, and it humbled her that her parents had sacrificed so much. They'd been the ones feeding and bathing her, taking her to doctor's appointments. They'd been desperate to find a way to get the nutrition she needed when she struggled to keep food down. They'd stood by helplessly as she fainted every time she attempted to stand up.

"I love you, Mom. Thank you for everything."

Her mom hugged her, and Peanut and her dad came into the room. The golden retriever's smiling face always put her in a good mood.

Dad rubbed his hands together. "I'll go pick up our dinner. We can eat it at the park."

"I'd rather eat it here if you don't mind." Ashlinn didn't want to worry about passing out in full view of anyone at the park. "I can come with you, though, to pick it up if you want company."

"That's okay. Stay here and rest." Her father patted his pockets for his keys. "You'll have your hands full after we leave."

That she would. While it made her nervous, she was looking forward to it. She'd make the most of her life while her health was good. Unless she had no other choice, she wouldn't move back in with her parents. For all their sakes, she hoped she wouldn't have to.

"A wiener dog? I didn't have that on my Bingo card for July." Cade handed Ty a large pizza box—still warm—then closed the front door and crouched to let Fritz sniff him. Their mother sailed down the hall ahead of them with her hands full of who knew what. Ty wasn't surprised to see his mom and brother here. For years, they'd been dropping in whenever the mood hit them. "I thought you were fostering a trainee. You know, a big dog."

"Change in plans." The aroma of pepperoni made his stomach growl. Ty carried the pizza to the kitchen and set it on the counter next to a box with a logo he recognized—Annie's Bakery. His mother might be a busybody, a terrible driver and a relentless matchmaker, but she also knew exactly what to bring to cheer him up. His taste buds came to life thinking about the doughnuts and cookies sure to be in the box.

"He's cute." Cade held the dog. Ty checked the pup's body language. Mouth relaxed and slightly opened. Ears alert. Tail wagging. Yep, the dog liked his brother. Not surprising. Everyone liked Cade, even dogs. "What's his name?"

"Fritz." After grabbing a stack of paper plates and some napkins from a cupboard, he set them on the counter. "Where's Mackenzie?"

"She got an emergency call. She had to drive out to the Yances' to check on one of their horses."

Ty admired that about Mackenzie. Her willingness to be on call 24/7. His sister-in-law had made an enormous impact on the surrounding area with her veterinary skills. Plus, she was genuine. No-frills. Ty got along well with her.

"Okay, my hands are free. Let me see your foster dog!" His mother rushed to Cade, who handed her the dog. "Oh, he is precious! Fritz, you said?"

The dog hadn't been here an hour, and Ty had already fallen head over heels for the little guy. The feeling seemed to be mutual, since he'd been following Ty everywhere.

"I'm so glad you're volunteering for Patrick." Mom stroked Fritz's back. "The training center helps so many people in need. And it's not easy for Patrick keeping up with all the expenses. Having you take a dog on the weekend is one less thing he needs to worry about."

Ty slid two slices on a plate and handed it to Cade. Then he dished out a slice for his mom. "Here you go, Ma."

"Thanks, hon. I could hold this sweetie all night long!" She turned to Fritz with the kissy face she reserved for small children and her dog, Tulip. "You are the cutest little thing. You're going to love it here. Don't worry if Ty gets grouchy. There's a softie lurking in those cowboy boots."

Ty and Cade exchanged wide-eyed glances and brought their plates to the kitchen table. A glass sliding door led to a patio, and the green grass of the back lawn ended in the distance at a split-log fence.

Their mother finally set down the dog and joined them at the table. After saying grace, they all dug into their pizza.

"Want anything to drink?" Ty wiped his mouth with a napkin, stood and headed to the door leading to the garage, where he kept a refrigerator for drinks.

"I'll take a diet soda," Mom said.

"I'll have whatever you're having," Cade said.

He opened the refrigerator, stacked three cans of soda and carried them back to the table. Once his mom and brother had their drinks, he returned to his chair, cracked open a Coke and took a long drink. Fritz stared up at him through big, begging eyes.

"No pizza for you, Fritzie." Ty smiled at the dog and patted his little head. He got excited and danced around the chair. "You've got kibble in your bowl."

"He needs a pepperoni." Their mom picked one off her pizza. It dangled between her manicured nails.

"No. Patrick said dachshunds are prone to overeating. I don't want him to become a literal sausage dog."

"Fine." She huffed, setting the pepperoni on her plate. She took a bite of crust. Ty gave it approximately one minute before she slipped the pepperoni to Fritz.

"How many weekends do you think you'll have him?" Cade grabbed a napkin from the holder in the center of the table.

"Probably just the one."

"You're not quitting already?" His mother's anguished tone and expression were as familiar to him as his face in the mirror. In the years since Zoey's death, his mother had been needling him to get out more, to spend time with friends, to join the Jewel River Legacy Club in town, to get a pet and most of all to "dip his toes in the dating pool."

"I'm not quitting. Patrick doesn't think Fritz is meant to

be a therapy dog anymore. The dog's been depressed since arriving at the center. He needs a permanent home, not an assignment."

"Little Fritzie's depressed?" His mom's lips wobbled. She wasn't going to cry, was she? "Poor little darling." She blinked a few times. Her chin rose. Alarm bells rang in his mind. "You have to adopt him, Ty."

Funny, he'd been thinking the same thing. But he couldn't. How had he gone from *Don't get attached* to *I want this dog forever* in the matter of an hour? It didn't make sense. And he wasn't ready to discuss it with his mother. He'd better change the subject.

"You mentioned Patrick's expenses with the center." Ty took another sip, watching his mom, who discreetly slid the forbidden pepperoni to the dog. The woman couldn't help herself. He couldn't imagine how badly she'd spoil grandchildren when Cade and Mackenzie started a family. "I thought the people who needed the service dogs paid for them."

"They do. The dogs are expensive. Thousands of dollars. To keep the clients' costs down, Patrick applies for grants. He occasionally gets donations, too."

"Hmm."

"What's that hmm for?" she asked.

"I've been thinking about Zoey—"

"It's time to let her go." Her tone sounded understanding, but something hard had infused it. His muscles tensed.

He'd never let Zoey go. She'd been the love of his life. He'd cherished her, and he would love her until the day he died. Living without her didn't really work. He merely existed. But even he could admit he'd hidden away on his ranch for too long. "I wasn't thinking...never mind."

"What were you thinking?" She brushed crumbs off her hands.

He shouldn't have said anything. Now his mom would get all up in his business—as usual—and he hadn't thought through what he wanted to do.

"Forget I said anything."

"No, go on. I want to hear." She tilted her head encouragingly.

He glanced at Cade, who gave him a look as if to say, *You got yourself into this.*

"I want to honor Zoey's memory."

Ty wasn't sure how he'd expected them to react, but it wasn't with silence. His mother typically filled every conversation gap from here to the next county.

"I think that's a nice idea." She nodded. "What are you thinking of doing?"

"I'm not sure." He turned his attention back to his plate. But with her mentioning how Patrick received funding, he might be able to combine the two.

"You could buy a memorial plaque," she said.

"I could." He didn't want to, though. Too sterile. "I'd like it to be more meaningful."

"Come to the Jewel River Legacy Club meeting. It's Tuesday night. Everyone will have plenty of suggestions for you." She'd asked him to attend one of the meetings no fewer than eight-hundred thousand times. He had a policy of avoiding contact with members of the community as much as possible. That way he could dodge awkward questions or pitying stares. "Or you could always wait until it's over and talk to Erica. With her owning the Winston, she's sure to have ideas."

That sounded more up his alley. Cade and Mackenzie's wedding reception had been at the Winston—a large pole barn converted to a rustic-inspired event center—on Erica Cambridge's ranch.

Wait. Was he actually considering going to the meeting? What was getting into him? Fostering a dog. Going to a meeting. What next—joining his mother's book club? He shuddered at the idea of all those romance novels.

"The meetings don't last long." Cade pushed back his chair and motioned for Ty to hand him his empty paper plate. He added his mom's to the pile and took them over to the trash can.

"Okay. I'll come. But only to talk to Erica."

Cade and Mom exchanged shocked glances.

"Good. And I'm serious about you adopting Fritz," Mom said. "He's happy here. And well behaved. Look."

Ty checked on him, and he was sitting next to his foot. He wagged his tail. The small dog positively tugged at his heart.

"I don't know…" Ty wanted Fritz, but he'd grow attached. And five or ten years down the line, the dog would die, and he'd be left with a broken heart all over again.

"I'll doggy-sit anytime. Tulip will *love* Fritz. Can you picture them together?" Mom brought her hand to the base of her throat. "It will be too adorable."

The Pomeranian *would* probably get along great with Fritz. They were about the same size. And knowing his mom would dog-sit eased his mind. "I'll think about it."

"Good." Her big smile made it seem like the matter was settled. Maybe it was. "Oh, I heard Patrick's new assistant arrived in town. I wonder what she's like."

"I met her." As soon as the words left his mouth, he regretted them. Now his mom would expect a thorough report about the new girl in town.

"You did?" Her voice lilted. "How old is she?"

"I don't know. I didn't ask." He gave Cade a stare that begged for help. But his traitor brother sat there grinning.

"Honestly, Ty, I don't need exact numbers." Exasperation poured from her. "Is she fresh out of high school? Your age? My age?"

"Younger than me." He barely got the words out through his clenched teeth. He knew exactly where this would go, and he wanted to kick himself for saying anything.

"Is she pretty?"

He let out a groan. The questions would be nonstop. Why had he opened his stupid mouth?

He'd better get everything out all at once. Then maybe… just maybe…his mother would leave him alone.

"She has a golden retriever wearing a service-dog vest. She's got blond hair. Blue eyes. She's real thin. Her name's Ashlinn." There. That should cover it.

Mom blinked rapidly.

"Don't ask me anything else. I barely met her." He pushed back his chair to toss his empty can into the recycling bin. Fritz's little toenails clicked rapidly behind him. He crouched to pet the dog. "Hey, buddy, are you keeping tabs on me?"

Those eyes pleaded for Ty to pick him up. Ty obliged, petting him all the way back to the table.

"I wonder if she's single…" Mom tapped a fingernail to her chin as she stared out at the back lawn. Ty held the dog close to his chest. *Here we go.*

Of course she would wonder if Ashlinn was single. Because his mother wasn't only a matchmaker, she was a meddler, too.

He never should have mentioned Ashlinn. It was bad enough he was considering adopting this dog. What would happen if he opened access to what he'd locked down long ago?

He'd be in big trouble. He couldn't let that happen.

No matchmaking. No girlfriends.

He'd be spending his life alone. Fritz licked his wrist.

Well, maybe not completely alone. He'd have to do some soul-searching before making a decision about adopting the dog. But there was no soul-searching necessary when it came to love. He'd done it once. He'd never fall in love again.

Chapter Two

When would this meeting end? Ty shifted in his seat again. It had been the longest two hours of his life, and the Jewel River Legacy Club members were still talking. His mom sat to his left, and Cade was at his right. If Mary Corning interrupted one more time with another bizarre idea—she'd actually mentioned buying drones to drop candygrams to citizens—he was getting up and leaving.

He'd survived the preview of the upcoming Shakespeare-in-the-Park film. To be fair, the movie, with its explosions and a tornado, appealed to him. Never having read Shakespeare, he doubted the original plays had so many explosions, but he could be wrong.

Ty had briefly considered raising his hand earlier to share his idea of hosting a fundraiser in Zoey's honor, but he'd chickened out. Having everyone hurl suggestions at him would have been horrible.

His mother was right—waiting for this to end so he could ask Erica Cambridge about it was the smart thing to do. And he'd already decided any money raised from the event would be donated to Howard Service Dogs. He couldn't think of a more worthy cause. He'd dropped Fritz off at the center yesterday morning, and he'd been thinking about the little dog constantly.

Did the dog miss him? Was he doing okay?

Everyone began to stand. Ty glanced around. He hadn't realized the meeting had ended. *Finally.*

"I'm getting ice cream with Clem." His mom patted Ty's hand. "Go catch Erica before she leaves."

"I'll see you later, bro." Cade put on his cowboy hat. "Mackenzie's waiting for me."

Ditched by his family. A first. They were the ones constantly harping on him to get out more and attend one of these meetings. He made his way over to Erica, the president of the club, as she slipped papers into a folder.

"Can I talk to you a minute, Erica?" Awkward didn't begin to describe the moment.

"Oh, hey, Ty. It's great to see you here. Are you thinking of joining the legacy club?" She gave him her full attention.

He shook his head. "Um, no. I'm thinking of hosting a fundraiser—"

"A fundraiser? Perfect!" She closed the folder and beamed. Erica was around his age. She'd moved to Jewel River a few years ago and married Dalton Cambridge. She'd been at the helm of helping bring the town back to its former glory. "Do you want to have it at the Winston?"

"I guess. If it's available." He scratched his chin, not sure what he was agreeing to. "I want it to honor Zoey Daniels. She was my fiancée. She died a long time ago." It felt strange saying all that. His throat tightened. Man, he missed her.

Erica's expression was all sympathy. "I know, and I'm sorry. I wish I could have met her."

"You'd have liked her." He knew deep down she would have, too.

"I'm sure."

"I want all the proceeds to go to Howard Service Dogs."

"Great idea!" She brought her hands together in the prayer

position below her chin. "You can host it at the Winston for free. Dalton and I want to help the service dog center as much as possible."

"Really?" He hadn't expected her generous response. "I couldn't let you do it for free. I'll pay to have the event there."

"No, you won't. It's for a good cause. You'll put on a dinner, right? What about hiring Drake Arless? He smokes a good barbecue. Oh! You could have silent auctions. Gift baskets and gift cards and all kinds of stuff. This is going to be amazing!"

Erica had certainly made it into a better idea than he could. "Sounds good."

"Why don't you call me tomorrow, and I'll let you know when the Winston has availability?"

"Okay," he said. "I don't have a date in mind. I'm pretty open."

"Good." She motioned for him to walk with her to the door. The community center had emptied out, and Dalton was waiting near the exit. "We tend to book up quickly, but we get cancellations, too. I'm sure we can find the perfect evening for it."

"All set?" Dalton asked after locking up. Erica filled him in on the fundraiser as the three of them strolled outside and across the parking lot. The sun was beginning to set. Another gorgeous summer evening in Wyoming.

Ty veered left toward his truck, and his mind went to Fritz. Yesterday morning, he'd told Patrick how active and happy Fritz had been all weekend. The doxie had adjusted to life with Ty in one second flat. Patrick thought maybe that was all the dog needed. A reminder that life wasn't over.

As much as he knew he shouldn't adopt the dog, he wanted to. If all it had taken for Fritz to bounce back was a weekend on his ranch, shouldn't he be glad? Then the dog would have a future helping someone else who needed him.

But Ty *wasn't* glad. Because *he* kind of needed him.

Patrick wanted to see how Fritz acted this week before making a decision. As long as the dog remained upbeat, Patrick would work with him until he could place him with a client.

Ty started the truck. Was it wrong to hope the dog didn't do well in training all week? He already missed him. Maybe he should have said something to Patrick about wanting to adopt Fritz. What if Patrick changed his mind and placed him with someone else before the week was over? Ty wouldn't be able to say goodbye.

On a whim, he turned in the opposite direction of his ranch to drive to the center. Yes, it was closed for the evening, but he didn't have anything else to do. A detour past it wouldn't hurt anyone.

As he neared the center, he noticed Ashlinn sitting on a patch of lawn near the sidewalk. She was petting the golden retriever, whose front legs were across her lap. Seemed odd. Why was she just sitting there? Did she need help?

He slowed the truck, pulled up in front of her and rolled down the window. "Everything okay?"

She blinked those big blue eyes up at him and nodded. "Yeah. Enjoying a walk."

Didn't look like much walking was getting done. "Do you need a ride?"

"No. I live two houses down." She angled her head in the direction of her house.

He wanted to ask why she was sitting on her neighbor's lawn if her house was so close. But it was none of his business. He put the truck in Drive but didn't take his foot off the brake.

"Are you settling in okay?" What was he doing? He'd

checked on her. She was fine. That meant he could drive away. But here he was, making small talk.

Ty didn't do small talk. He should leave.

"Yes, Peanut's been a big help."

The dog stretched across her lap did *not* look like he was helping, but what did Ty know?

"I'm glad. Well, I'll see you around."

"See you later." She kept petting the dog. He eased off the brake and drove past the center. When he turned around to head back, Ashlinn was walking the dog up her porch steps.

Good. She seemed fine. No need for him to worry.

But he did worry. A little. Because that dog was wearing a service-dog vest for a reason, and something told him Ashlinn hadn't been sitting in the neighbor's yard on a whim.

She'd been dreaming of having a job—a purpose—and her dream had finally come true. On Thursday afternoon, Ashlinn took a break from entering Patrick's client contact information into a spreadsheet. She'd been at the center for almost two hours. The first hour had involved greeting the dogs and letting them get used to her. The second hour had been working on the paperwork Patrick had let pile up, including organizing client forms and what type of dog they needed. They'd agreed it was a long-term project she would work on only when she felt up to it.

Today she felt up to it—at least she had earlier. Now? She was getting tired. Peanut had curled up on a dog bed in the corner of the office. Every now and then he came over to check on her, and then he'd wander back to the bed. She was thankful he'd only had to alert her twice, and both times, she'd reclined on the floor and hadn't passed out.

Patrick appeared in the doorway. "Question for you."

"What is it?"

"Fritz." He bent down and scooped up the miniature dachshund Ty had fostered last weekend. "I keep hoping he'll come around, but he's not acclimating here. He's mopey again. Tomorrow, I'm going to call around to find him a home. In the meantime, I think Fritz could use a lap to sit on. Are you up for it?"

"Am I up for it?" She beamed and held out her arms. "I would love to have him on my lap."

Peanut woke and, tail wagging, joined them. Patrick set Fritz on the floor. The dogs sniffed each other, and the way their tails were wagging, she assumed they liked each other. Peanut came over to sniff her and sauntered away. She took the opportunity to pick up Fritz. As she petted him, he licked the back of her hand a few times, then settled on her lap and let out an exhausted sigh.

"You're tired, aren't you?" she said to Fritz as she glanced at Patrick, who was taking a binder off a shelf. "I hate to think of him all sad and out of sorts."

"Me, too." He opened the binder and flipped through the pages. "Wish I could place him with a client. From all accounts, he did wonders for his previous owner's depression and anxiety. It's a shame he won't be able to help someone else who needs him."

"At least he helped one person," she said softly. "He could come home with me tonight if you think it would help. I don't like thinking of him here all sad."

"I appreciate the offer, but we don't know how he'd do with Peanut, and you have enough to deal with. I'm going to give Ty a call. Fritz was a completely different dog with him last weekend. I'll see if he'll keep him until I can find someone to adopt him."

Ty. She'd thought about the handsome cowboy too many times over the past few days. She hadn't even been here a week. How could he have taken up so much space in her head already?

Probably because he liked dogs, had volunteered to foster Fritz last weekend and had stopped to check on her the other night when she'd had an episode.

Had she been embarrassed that he'd pulled up to find her sitting on a stranger's patch of grass? Yes. Had she told him the reason why she'd been sitting there? No.

If only she'd been able to make it home before Peanut had started licking her hand…but no. And it wasn't as if she'd had other options. Peanut had broken out of his heel and blocked her from going any farther. The dog had known her blood pressure was plummeting. And when she'd sat on the grass, her shallow breathing and erratic pulse had confirmed it. She'd been dangerously close to passing out. By the time Ty had pulled up, she'd been almost back to normal. Almost.

Seeing his handsome face and hearing the concern in his tone had affected her blood pressure in the opposite way, and it had nothing to do with her autoimmune disease.

She was attracted to the cowboy. Plain and simple. He seemed like a genuine, kind guy.

"I'm going to call him now." Patrick left, and Ashlinn absentmindedly petted the sleeping dog. Peanut came over, wagging his tail, and checked on both of them before going back to the bed. She saved her progress in the spreadsheet and began shutting down the program. Time to call it a day.

Her phone rang, and when she saw who was calling, she answered it. "Hi, Dad."

"How's it going, kiddo?" He and her mom called multiple times each day, and she always tried to answer as soon as she could. Didn't want to worry them.

"I'm good. I'm at the center, typing in a spreadsheet."

"Don't overdo it."

"I'm not. I'm actually wrapping up. Oh, and I've got a mini-doxie on my lap. He's so cute."

"A wiener dog?" His voice grew animated. "I had one of those growing up."

"He's feeling displaced at the moment. Patrick's working on finding him a home."

"Well, it makes me feel better knowing you've got a dog on your lap. Means you're sitting."

She chuckled. "Trust me, I force myself to sit. You don't think I'm over here running laps, do you?"

"I hope not." He laughed. "Any episodes?"

"The usual." She slowly stroked Fritz's back. "Nothing Peanut and I couldn't handle."

"What about getting around? Were your groceries delivered? Did you find a ride to church?"

"I'm getting around fine. And I'm not ready for church." She wasn't ready to be out and about at all. Just living by herself and walking to work a few days a week were massive changes she'd need time to get used to.

"All right. I wanted to make sure you're taking care of yourself and not working too much."

"I know. I'm doing my best."

"Go right back home and get in bed if you need to. Get in bed whenever you need to."

"I will." They'd been over this a thousand times. "But I don't need to be in bed right now. I'm sitting in the office with a sweet little dog on my lap and Peanut in the corner. I'm fine."

"If you need us to come up there, say the word. And if you want to move back home, we'll make it happen."

She rolled her eyes. "Da-a-d."

"You can't blame me for caring."

"I don't. But let me try to be independent, okay?"

"We're trying."

"Listen, Dad, I've got to go."

"Call me when you get home."

She ended the call. She might be living in a different state, but some things never changed. Her parents' concern for her could feel overbearing at times. She tried not to resent it. At least they cared.

Patrick came back into the office. "Ty's on his way."

"You mean I have to give up my lap warmer?" She faked a frown.

He chuckled. "He's at his mother's place here in town, so you've got five or ten minutes with a warm lap. I'm going to start feeding the dogs." He knocked his knuckles on the doorframe and left.

Five or ten minutes. That should give her time to calm the chaos in her tummy. As if on cue, Peanut came over and licked the back of her hand.

"I know, buddy, but trust me, this isn't a fainting thing." She ruffled his fur, and with his tongue lolling, he strolled away. She had enough physical issues. She certainly didn't need to add romantic flutters to the list of things Peanut alerted to.

And anyhow, the cowboy was off-limits. Her life had shrunk six years ago. Sure, it might have gone up a size over the past year, but that didn't mean she could fit a boyfriend into it.

She was too scared to go to church or enter a store. She could only work four or five hours a week—if that. And she'd fainted at least twice every day since moving here.

Ashlinn wasn't in any shape to have a boyfriend, and she wouldn't torture herself into thinking she was. A yawn caught hold, and she took a deep breath. As soon as Ty came for Fritz, she and Peanut were heading home.

Chapter Three

Ty made it to the training center in four minutes flat. His mom had been getting on his nerves anyhow. She'd gone on and on about how Ty should invite Ashlinn to church. When he'd grunted to indicate there was no way he was doing that, she'd shoved a book in his hand—some romance novel that he'd dropped faster than the rhinestone-covered cowboy hat she'd handed him while shopping last fall—and basically commanded him to give Ashlinn the book and to tell her about book club.

He'd tap-dance on Broadway before that would happen.

His mother could browbeat Ashlinn into coming to the book club herself. He wanted no part of it. He'd been around more people this week than he had in the previous year. Made him want to pitch a tent in the mountains by his lonesome for a month—with Fritz, of course.

Ty couldn't wait to see the dog again. And this time, he wasn't taking chances. He was coming right out and asking Patrick if he could adopt Fritz. He hoped the man agreed. Ty parked the truck, pocketed his keys and took long strides to the entrance.

Barking from the kennel area grabbed his attention, but he didn't see Patrick over there. Ty strolled to the office and paused in the doorway. Fritz was asleep on Ashlinn's lap.

Her tender expression as she petted him reminded him of a young mother with her baby. Punched him right in the gut.

Since when had he gotten so sentimental? Ashlinn must have sensed him there because she smiled at him.

"I suppose I have to give him up, huh?" Her eyes shimmered with good humor. A guy would get lost in those ocean-blue eyes.

Ocean eyes? What was wrong with him? It was that romance novel. The brief contact with it had turned him into a sap. He needed to haul himself back to the ranch. Ride a horse. Rope a calf. Pitch some hay.

"Is Patrick around?" Why did his voice sound like he'd swallowed gravel?

"He's feeding the dogs. Check the kennel room."

He nodded, wanting to say something more, but not trusting himself to say anything coherent. He wandered toward the kennels and found Patrick scratching behind Charger's ears as the rest of the dogs ate their kibble.

"Thanks for coming, Ty. Let's go to the office. Fritz is in there with Ashlinn."

Ty fell in beside him as they crossed the main training area.

"Fritz isn't adjusting here." Patrick gave him a sideways glance. "I'm disappointed, but I've got to do what's right for him. I think it's time to place him in a permanent home— as a pet. I'm wondering if you'd keep him with you on the ranch until I find him a new owner. I don't want him miserable here when he could be enjoying life."

Ty's heart pounded in his chest. "I'll take him. Permanently."

Patrick halted, clearly taken aback. "You want Fritz?"

"Yeah. He fit right into my life last weekend. I like the dog. I think he'll be happy with me."

"I know he'll be happy." Patrick grinned, shaking his head. "I'm surprised. You were adamant about only wanting a dog on the weekends."

"I know." He shrugged, the corner of his mouth kicking up. "Surprised me, too. Fritz is special, and I hope you'll agree to let me adopt him."

"Of course you can adopt him. Can't think of a better placement for the dog."

Fritz was his! What a fantastic development.

"There's something else I want to run past you, too." He'd been meaning to talk to Patrick about the fundraiser, and now was as good a time as any.

"What is it?"

"I believe in what you're doing here. I admire all the hard work you put into training these dogs. They'll help people lead fuller lives."

"They sure will. And thanks. I love my job."

"It's obvious," Ty said. "A long time ago, I was engaged to a local girl named Zoey Daniels. She passed away from cystic fibrosis before we could get married. She'd appreciate what you're doing here, too."

"I'm sorry for your loss." His sympathetic expression matched his tone.

"I want to host a fundraiser dinner in Zoey's honor with all the proceeds going to Howard Service Dogs."

"You're serious?" Patrick looked stunned, then his face lit up. "I don't know what to say. Thank you. I've been trying to figure out how to purchase a wheelchair-accessible transit van to pick up our clients from the airport. This will jump-start a down payment."

"Any money from the event can go straight toward it." Ty was humbled he could provide something concrete for such a worthy cause. Zoey would approve.

"Three dogs will be fully trained and ready to be placed with their owners this fall. And after Brooke Dewitt gets married to Dean McCaffrey in September, she's going to let my clients rent her house—it's fully accessible for wheelchairs—so they can spend a week here while I train them how to handle their dogs. Getting the clients from the airport to Jewel River was the only problem I hadn't resolved."

"In that case, I'd better make sure the fundraiser is soon. Erica Cambridge offered to host it at the Winston. The earliest opening she has available is the second Friday in September. I'll ask her to save it for me."

"That's great." Patrick shook Ty's hand vigorously. "Wow, I appreciate this, Ty."

They continued to make their way to the office, discussing the type of van Patrick wanted to buy. Barking loudly, Fritz raced out the door to them. Patrick immediately jogged ahead, and Ty picked up the dog. Fritz laser-focused on the office and barked nonstop.

Something must be wrong. When Ty made it inside, his heart dropped to the floor.

Ashlinn was flat on her back near the dog bed, and her golden retriever was nudging her limp hand and licking her palm and wrist. She was clearly unconscious.

"Oh, dear." Patrick kneeled next to her. "Hey, Ashlinn, wake up."

His voice was quiet, calm, whereas Ty had gone straight to panic mode. What should he do? She needed help. He set Fritz on the floor—the dog trotted straight to Peanut and Ashlinn—and grabbed the cell phone from his pocket.

"I'll call 911," he said.

"No need." Patrick stood. "She's coming to."

"But she's on the floor. She fainted or had a heart attack

or…" His breath seized in his lungs. He had no idea what had happened.

"She passed out. This happens regularly. She'll be fine."

This happened regularly? Ty tried to make sense of it and couldn't.

Ashlinn came to and groggily started petting the golden retriever. "Good boy. Good job, Peanut." The dog stayed near her as she reached for a water bottle. She sat up enough to take a long drink. Fritz sniffed her, then turned away to go straight to Ty.

Once again, he picked up the dog, but this time, he cradled him to his chest and petted him. Seeing her on the floor had given him a scare. Fritz licked his forearm as he stroked his back.

Ashlinn slowly rose to a seated position, and it was only then that Ty realized a folded blanket covered her calves, and she'd had her head on a pillow. It was as if she'd prepared ahead of time. She seemed to realize Ty was in the room, and her face flushed.

"You okay, Ash?" Patrick asked in a normal tone. "Need me to get you anything?"

"I'm okay." She shook her head, glancing sideways at Ty. "Sorry you had to see that."

See what? He wanted to know what was going on.

But it was none of his business.

"I don't know if Patrick told you, but I have AAG, Autoimmune Autonomic Ganglionopathy. Say that three times fast." She let out an embarrassed chuckle, still looking exhausted. "It means I pass out often. Among other things."

AAG. An autoimmune disorder. His mind skipped back to when he'd met Zoey. How she'd warned him she had cystic fibrosis, and he'd told her he didn't care, he just wanted to be with her.

Knowing what he knew now, he wouldn't put himself through that with another woman.

"I'm sorry to hear that." He continued petting Fritz, who finally stopped licking him. The tail end of her comment caught up with him. *Among other things.* What other things?

"Peanut alerts me when my blood pressure gets low. He always knows when I'm going to pass out. It gives me time to get to a safe position. That's why I was sitting on the lawn the other day."

"Your blood pressure got low."

"Yep." She moved to stand up, and Patrick thrust his hand out to help her. She took it, and when she was upright, placed her palm on the desk to steady herself.

"Ty's adopting Fritz." Patrick gave her the water bottle. "And he's hosting a fundraiser for this place. The van might not be a wish much longer."

Her face took on a healthy glow. "That's wonderful! Fritz will be happy with you. And a fundraiser—how generous. I'd love to help."

"Um, thank you, I've got it under control." He didn't have it under control at all. Honestly, he had no clue what needed to be done. Erica had mentioned hiring Drake for barbecue and something about an auction, but beyond that he didn't know what was required.

"Oh." Disappointment covered her face. "Okay."

Now he felt like a jerk, turning down her offer.

Patrick opened a file cabinet behind the desk and took out a manilla folder. "Here's everything you need for Fritz. The papers show he's a purebred miniature dachshund. You'll see the list of all his shots, his Canine Good Citizen certificate and notes regarding his previous home."

"Thank you." Ty set Fritz down to leaf through the papers. "What do I need to do?"

"Fill out a form with the county to get him licensed. That's it."

"What about an adoption fee?"

"None for you. Oh, and feel free to take Fritz to the nursing home when you visit your grandmother. Just put a therapy-dog vest on him first." Patrick patted him on the shoulder, then turned to Ashlinn. "Why don't I take you home? Then you won't have to walk. I know it's been a long day."

Ty could see in her expression she was going to decline. He felt bad for dismissing her help with the fundraiser. "It's on my way. I'll drop you off. And Peanut, of course."

"Great," Patrick said. "Then I can let out the dogs again."

Ty turned to Ashlinn. "Ready?"

"You don't have to do that." He couldn't read her body language. But he knew he'd been the one to dull her glow. And he remembered how Zoey had wished people wouldn't see her as incapable. Regret piled on at dismissing Ashlinn's offer.

"It's on my way. I'll feel better if you'll let me."

She sighed and nodded. "Let me get my things together."

A sense of victory overcame him. And that in itself was disturbing. It seemed no matter what he told himself was the right thing to do, lately, he did the opposite. And with a woman like Ashlinn, that could be costly. But what choice did he have? He couldn't let her walk home after passing out. He'd keep an emotional distance. He'd been perfecting it for six years.

Ashlinn fumbled, dropping her keys, as she attempted to unlock her front door. Today couldn't get any more embarrassing. Ty stood directly behind her, holding Fritz's leash, and Peanut was by her side. She'd told Ty she didn't need him walking her to the door, but apparently, he'd thought otherwise.

He probably viewed her as an invalid, unable to fend for herself. In some ways, he'd be correct.

She'd been mortified to have him witness her fainting spell earlier. Sure, the incidents barely fazed her after all these years. But she'd never had someone she was attracted to witness her passing out. Until today.

And the fact it had been Ty made her mortification so much worse. What a thoughtful man. Putting on a fundraiser. Adopting Fritz. Insisting on driving her home.

Ty bent and picked up the keys before she had a chance to. His fingers grazed hers as he handed them to her. How could a simple touch make her feel all swoony? "Here you go."

Even his deep voice was giving her junior-high-crush vibes. It had been a long time since she'd been around a cute guy and even longer since she'd dated one. None of her previous dates could hold a candle to Ty, though.

"Thanks." This time the key fit in the lock, and she opened the door.

"About the fundraiser..." he said. She turned back to him. "I *could* use some help. But only if you want to. I mean, you might have offered just to be nice."

He wanted her help? Maybe he didn't see her as an invalid after all.

"I'd love to help." She hesitated. Should she invite him in? This was all new to her—having her own place, being independent in a new town. "Want to talk about it now?"

He checked on Fritz, who stood at his feet smiling up at him with his little tongue panting. "Sure. If you don't mind Fritz being with me."

"Please. I adore him." She headed inside with Peanut,

and Ty and Fritz joined her. She promptly got to one knee to remove Peanut's vest. Then she hugged him and scratched behind his ears. Rising, she nodded to the couch. "Make yourself at home. Do you want anything to drink?"

"No thanks." He found a seat. She dropped into her favorite chair and closed her eyes briefly to get her bearings. Peanut went to the kitchen. Fritz took off in his direction. The sound of lapping water reached her.

"I'll make sure he doesn't get into anything." Ty rose and left the room.

Maybe she shouldn't have offered to assist with the fundraiser. She'd put in two hours of work today and felt like she could sleep for a week. She wouldn't be surprised if she had another fainting episode tonight. Moving to a new town and starting a job might not be a big deal for someone else her age, but for her? She was nearing the outer limits of her energy levels—and stress ramped up her symptoms.

What if she relapsed and ended up bedridden again?

"Guess I worried for nothing." Ty returned with Fritz on his heels. Peanut wasn't far behind. "Do you care if he sits up here with me?"

"Of course not. Have at it."

Ty sat down again, this time with Fritz on his lap. The dog circled twice to get comfortable. "About the fundraiser…"

"Right. When is it?" She glanced around for her water bottle. She kept water on hand at all times. It helped her manage the fainting better. "Excuse me. I need to get some water."

"I'll get it," he said.

"No, no. I'm fine." She took her time rising. "Don't want to disturb the tired little puppy."

He chuckled. "He's pretty worn out."

"I'm glad you're adopting him. He's a completely different dog with you than at the center." She left the room and poured water into a drink tumbler, then returned to her seat. She should have grabbed a bag of potato chips. Not only was she getting hungry, the salt helped raise her blood pressure.

"How long have you had AAG?" Ty asked.

She schooled her face, not wanting to reveal her surprise that he remembered what her disease was called.

"Six years."

The way he startled confused her. Was she missing something?

"Six years ago I was supposed to get married, but my fiancée passed away before the big day. Cystic fibrosis."

"I'm so sorry." She brought her hand to her chest. The poor man. "I guess it was a bad year for both of us."

"I guess so." He met her gaze, and the warmth in it made her stomach swirl. "The fundraiser will be in her honor. Her name was Zoey Daniels."

A sinking feeling came over her. Was he still in love with the woman? Zoey?

Of course he was still in love with her. Why else would he host a fundraiser in her name?

"That's a lovely thing to do," she said quietly. Inside, though, her heart hurt. She didn't see herself ever getting to a point where she could have a long-term relationship. Her health problems were too limiting for her to date someone.

No one would ever host a dinner in her memory. No one would get close enough to her to want to.

Shame crushed her. How awful—to be jealous of a dead woman. At least Ashlinn could be thankful she wouldn't be dying anytime soon. "Where are you at with the planning?"

"I'm not far." He had the look of a man in over his head. "I need to call Erica—Erica Cambridge owns the event center—and let her know the twelfth of September works. It's a Friday. That should be okay, right?"

"Friday seems like a good time for a dinner." Her gaze strayed to Peanut. He was lounging in his dog bed and nibbling on one of his back paws. Good. That meant she wasn't having issues.

"She recommended a local who caters barbecue. I guess I need to call him. Beyond that, I don't know."

"Ask Erica if we need to provide tablecloths and paper plates, napkins, that sort of thing. We'll also have to create flyers and find a way to get the word out around town."

"I didn't think of all that." His eyes, deep brown, met hers. "Oh, she mentioned a silent auction."

"Good idea." Ashlinn was beginning to picture the event. She'd helped plan school dances in high school, and she'd been in a sorority before having to drop out of college due to her illness. Planning events was in her blood. "We'll contact local businesses and any groups or clubs to see if they'll donate items for it."

"They'll do that?"

"They sure will." She nodded. "What about an emcee?"

His shoulders climbed to his ears as he shook his head. "I'm not the person to ask."

"Does Zoey have family around?"

"Not here. Her parents moved to Colorado to be near her brother."

"We can figure out an emcee and everything else later. We have plenty of time. Almost two months." She yawned, trying to stifle it with her palm, but failing. "Sorry about that."

"Don't be." He picked up Fritz and stood. "I should get going."

"I wasn't trying to run you off."

"I know." He hesitated. "This is a weird question, but you obviously walk to work. Do you have a car?"

"No. I can't get a driver's license with my health the way it is."

"Oh." He averted his eyes. "If you need a ride to church or wherever, let me know. In fact, if you need anything, holler. I'll give you my number."

There went her tummy again, twirling like batons in a marching band. She'd have to remind herself later that he was offering out of kindness. Best not to read more into it. She swiped her phone. "What's your number?"

He spelled out his full name and his number. Then she texted him: This is Ashlinn Burnier.

Soon, she'd followed him to the front door and said goodbye to Fritz. Then she gripped the door handle.

"You sure you're okay?" His caring voice wiggled into the lonely part of her she tended to ignore. How easy it would be to ask him to stay.

But she couldn't. She'd help with the fundraiser, and by the time September rolled around, Ty would have plenty of opportunities to see she lived a very limited life. She'd never put a man into such a tiny box. But she was thankful for her tiny box, just the same.

"I'm okay." She gave him what she hoped passed for a smile.

He searched her eyes, then glanced down at Fritz. "All right. See you around."

Yes, she'd see him around. And fight the envy that some other girl would get to date this cowboy and have all the things her disease had taken from her.

She'd better get out her Bible. Envy was an ugly look on her. And she didn't intend on wearing it for long.

What a day. Ty buckled Fritz into the booster seat, then loped around the front of the truck to climb into the driver's side. He now owned a dog. And he'd agreed to let a beautiful woman with major health problems help him plan the dinner he was hosting in honor of his dead fiancée.

Life was strange.

As he put the truck in Reverse and checked the mirrors, a sense of hope filled him, though. He was doing the right thing, having Ashlinn help him.

She clearly knew what needed to be done, and he didn't. Plus, he'd realized another way he could honor Zoey. She'd always wanted to be treated like everyone else. Ashlinn probably did, too. He regretted treating her like an invalid earlier.

Soon he was speeding down the country road to his ranch. The mountains in the distance always made him feel like he was part of something bigger than his own life. The vast prairies on either side of the road were beautiful in the summer. *He maketh me to lie down in green pastures.* Psalm 23. Funny that one came to mind.

Ashlinn couldn't drive. She fainted on a regular basis.

Among other things.

He didn't know what those other things entailed, but something told him she wouldn't be straying far from home, and it wasn't by choice. Her world was a within-walking-distance one. And since she passed out often, she couldn't be walking far.

He was going to do something about that. He'd invite her to church like his mother suggested. Bring her out to the ranch so she could see the beauty of Wyoming for herself.

Maybe he could expand her within-walking-distance life a little bit.

As long as he protected his heart, he'd be okay. And it wouldn't be difficult. All he had to do was picture Zoey's smiling face. It wasn't possible for him to love anyone else. Not even the new girl in town with pretty blue eyes and a big heart to match.

Chapter Four

Would the dogs be able to detect blood pressure abnormalities by being around her? The following Wednesday, Ashlinn sat in the training arena while the two dogs Patrick had acquired over the weekend sniffed her. Bandit, the German shepherd, had a lot of energy. The golden-retriever-basset-hound mix, Candy, had just finished a fourteen-month stint with a puppy trainer and showed promise to be a service dog.

At the beginning of the session, Patrick had swabbed Ashlinn's saliva and allowed both dogs to smell it. Her blood pressure readings remained steady. Surprising, seeing how much she'd been looking forward to this afternoon. Ty was picking her up soon to discuss the plans for the event.

"The more we get them used to your scent when your blood pressure is normal, the easier it will be for them to recognize the chemical reactions altering it when it's low." Patrick allowed them to linger another minute and led them to the corner before commanding them to sit and stay. He came back over to her. "I think that should do it. I know you've got your meeting with Ty. Why don't you get your things together and call it a day?"

"Are you sure? I can stick around a few more minutes. Maybe my blood pressure will change."

"No, go on. We'll have many opportunities over the next

months." Patrick turned back to the dogs. She stood, and a whoosh of dizziness came over her. Peanut immediately licked her hand. She sat right back down. "Bring them over, Patrick. I feel lightheaded."

He brought both dogs to her. Bandit's nose traveled from her hand to her thigh and feet. He spun in a circle once. Patrick rewarded him with a treat. Candy barely paid any attention to her. The dog plopped down on the mat, bringing her hind leg up to itch her ear.

"She doesn't seem interested." Ashlinn nodded to Candy.

"That might change."

She checked her blood pressure. Almost back to normal. Good. "I'm going to try this again. Do you want them both near me just in case?"

"Yeah, let's see what happens." He called the dogs to come.

She took her time rising. Peanut moseyed over. Bandit did, too. He smelled her once and walked away, the same as Peanut. That was a good sign. Candy plunked down on the mat, not interested in her at all.

"I think Bandit shows promise. We'll see about Candy. It's too early to tell at this point." Patrick walked out of the training area with her. "Thank you for being patient with them."

"I'm happy to do it. I don't know what my life would look like without Peanut, but I do know this. I wouldn't be here, living on my own. I hope both Bandit and Candy can be trained to help someone else live more independently. You're doing God's work here, Patrick."

"I hope the same, and thank you. I'm blessed to love what I do."

The entrance doors opened, and Ty strolled in with Fritz by his side. The dachshund picked up speed as he saw Patrick, Ashlinn and Peanut.

"Heel, Fritz," Ty said. The dog immediately fell in beside him and stopped straining at the leash. "Good boy."

Ashlinn's heartbeat thumped in anticipation. She'd talked to Ty twice since he'd dropped her off at her house last week, and she'd been looking forward to seeing him tonight. Peanut's nose brushed her hand. She almost chuckled. The dog knew.

"How's Fritz doing?" Patrick checked over his shoulder—Bandit and Candy were fine—and bent to pet Fritz.

"Great. I've been getting him used to the horses and the stables. He might be under the impression he was born to be a herding dog." His eyes shimmered with humor.

"Small in body," Ashlinn said. "Big in personality."

"Exactly." Ty met her gaze, and she almost fanned herself. Peanut stayed close by. She patted his head. Couldn't fault the dog for knowing her inside and out.

"Do you think you'd be up for fostering one of the dogs occasionally on the weekends still? Not this weekend, of course, but maybe in a few weeks." Patrick gave Fritz's back a final stroke and straightened.

"I hadn't thought about it." With his free hand, Ty wiped his forehead beneath his cowboy hat. "I probably could."

"Great. Bandit, especially, could use a break running around your property. He's still a puppy at heart."

"I've got plenty of land for him to explore." Ty glanced at Ashlinn again, and she had to force herself to look away.

She excused herself to get her bag and Peanut's harness from the office. When she returned and got the dog situated, they chatted another minute before saying goodbye. Ty held the door open for her and Peanut, then he and Fritz accompanied her to his truck. He helped her into the passenger seat. After getting Fritz and Peanut settled in the backseat, he started the truck and turned to her. "If you want a change of scenery, we could go to my ranch."

She instantly pictured horses in pastures with mountains behind them. Wouldn't it be something to see his ranch in person? But she wasn't ready. Might never be ready.

"It's about a thirty-minute drive." He waited patiently for her answer.

"Um, I don't think that's a good idea." She didn't want to offend him. "It has nothing to do with your ranch. It's just… I'm safer at home."

He nodded. "I get that. You should come out at some point, though. If you need me to have anything on hand to make it safer for you, let me know. I've got a great view of the mountains, and the prairie spreads for miles. There's no better place to see the sunset than from my front porch."

The way he described it was exactly how she imagined it. While she'd love to visit, it wouldn't be wise. Not now, anyway. "Wyoming sunsets are pretty spectacular."

"They sure are." He didn't seem put out by her refusal. "Your place, then?"

"Yes." As he drove, Ashlinn's thoughts circled around. Ty wasn't a pressure guy. Nothing about the exchange made her feel like she'd disappointed him. But a part of her disappointed herself. She hadn't even realized she wanted to see his ranch until he'd invited her. And she'd turned him down—she'd done the right thing, hadn't she?

He pulled into her driveway and parked. "Wait there. I'll come around."

A chivalrous cowboy. Maybe it was only due to her disease, but something about Ty made her believe he'd open the door for her regardless of her health status.

"Thanks." She took his hand to step down. Calloused skin. His touch sent a tiny thrill through her veins. He let go as soon as she was out of the truck. Truthfully, though, she wouldn't mind if he held her hand all the way inside.

"I'll get the dogs."

Ashlinn waited for Peanut to get out of the truck, then she climbed the porch steps and unlocked the front door. Ty brought Fritz inside. Ashlinn crouched to remove Peanut's harness, giving him a lot of loving as she did. When she straightened, he and Fritz gravitated to each other. Ty had taken off his cowboy hat.

"Want some iced tea?" she asked on her way to the kitchen. "I brewed it myself on the porch."

"Sun tea? I'd love a glass."

"Coming right up." She took two glasses out of the cupboard and filled them with ice from the fridge's dispenser. After pouring the tea, she brought the glasses to the living room and handed one to Ty. "Did you want a snack, too? My groceries were delivered yesterday."

"No, I'm good. Is the delivery working out for you?"

"Yes. They leave everything on my front porch. All I have to do is put it all away. My parents were relieved when I told them it went well. That was one of their biggest concerns about me moving here. How would I get food?"

"Yeah, we aren't like the city where you can have everything delivered. At least we have the supermarket and Cowboy John's for local delivery." He sipped the tea. "This is good. What flavor is it?"

"It's my favorite. Ginger peach." She took a drink and leaned back in her chair.

"Long day?" he asked.

"No. But a good day. Patrick started getting the new dogs used to my scent. We'll be working with them for the foreseeable future to detect when my blood pressure changes.

It's exciting, thinking someone like me will have a dog of their own to help them."

"It is," he said so quietly she almost didn't hear it.

She reached into the basket next to her chair and pulled out a notebook and pen. After turning to the page with her notes for the event, she turned her attention back to Ty, who'd lifted Fritz to the couch. The dog was in the process of curling up on his lap. "Why don't you tell me where you're at with the planning?"

"Sure." He set the glass on a coaster. "Erica reserved the Winston for me on September twelfth. We'll be able to set up the day before, and she gave me the number of a cleanup crew to hire if we don't want to do it ourselves."

"Did you find out if we'll need tablecloths and stuff like that?"

"I did. She'll provide tablecloths, disposable dinnerware, glasses and napkins—all for a fee."

Ashlinn frowned. "Will we be able to afford it?"

"Yes. Erica and Dalton are donating the Winston for the dinner. No charge. I'm covering the costs of everything else."

"And then we'll pay you back from the proceeds." She added bullet points in her notebook.

"No. I don't want repayment. Like I said, this is to help Patrick. Knowing he'll be one step closer to purchasing that van makes me feel good."

His generosity made her hand falter. Throwing a big fundraiser like this would cost thousands of dollars—money Ty could use for any number of things.

"Why?" She stopped writing to stare at him, trying to figure him out. "Besides honoring Zoey?"

He averted his eyes, and his knee began to bounce. Then he met her gaze. "I don't have the expenses a lot of guys my age deal with. No wife or wedding to pay for. No kids and all the costs they entail. I live a simple life. And I don't think God intended for me to hoard His blessings."

She found his contentment refreshing. In many ways, she and Ty were similar. Except she had a solid reason for not having all the things he'd listed. Why didn't he have a wife or children?

"You say that like you don't ever plan on having a wife or kids."

"I don't."

She was taken aback. Maybe she shouldn't press for more information, but she couldn't help herself. "I'm not getting married or having kids, either. I know my reasons. What are yours?"

His face flushed. "There was only one Zoey. And she's gone."

The words pricked her heart. Of course. She'd figured as much. Why a teeny part of her had hoped otherwise, she wouldn't think about. Zoey had been his one true love.

"What about you?" He tilted his head, curiosity written all over his face.

"I'm…this…" she motioned her hand down her body "…is my life. I wouldn't put a husband through it."

"Is your condition terminal?"

"No," she shook her head, "AAG won't cut my days short." It would just make them difficult.

"What all are you dealing with?" His concerned tone didn't demand answers, but she figured it couldn't hurt to be honest.

"The fainting, obviously. Dizziness. I get tired easily. Stomach issues—a lot of stomach issues. Sometimes I struggle with dry mouth. Dry eyes. There are times when I can't sleep. And on rare occasions, I'll get confused. It's like a mental fog. But that's more if I have a migraine."

"I'm sorry. That must be difficult for you."

"I'm much better now than I was a year ago." She kept her tone bright, not wanting him to think she was feeling sorry for herself. "I mean, look at me. I have my own house and a part-time job. Peanut." The dog glanced up from his dog bed. "You're the best dog in the world, aren't you, boy?"

"I'm glad." He leaned back with a tender, understanding expression. "And since you're doing better, I think we should plan a time for you to come out and see my ranch."

"I don't think so." She drew her eyebrows together. "My health…"

"We'll make a fainting station for you."

"But the other things I deal with—"

"If you're having a bad day, we'll reschedule."

She was finding it hard to turn him down. And her earlier vision of endless prairie made her not want to. "Why do you want me there?"

"I know it must be hard being home or at the center all the time."

"Not really. I feel like I'm on vacation compared to the years I spent in bed, only leaving the house to see the doctor."

"I won't push you. I'll drop the subject." He stretched his neck to one side then the other. "I promise I'm not a creeper."

"I didn't peg you for one." She let out a small laugh. It was curious that a man so stuck on his deceased fiancée was insisting she come out to see his ranch. Maybe it was pity, but she didn't think so.

"If you ever change your mind…"

As much as she'd like to see his land, she wasn't changing her mind. This house, her job—they were enough for her. And if she continued to decline his invitations, at some point Ty would give up on her, which would be for the best.

She might not like it, but staying in her world gave her the best chance to continue to live independently.

"We should get back to the planning," she said.

"Planning. Right." Ty's neck burned. Why had he pressed Ashlinn to visit his ranch? He shouldn't have been so heavy-handed. She clearly didn't want to, and why would she? Her health problems kept her close to home. Going someplace new would probably be too stressful for her.

The fact he'd even invited her would be laughable to anyone who knew him well. He was an expert at avoiding people. He'd been hibernating for six years.

With a quick scan of his list, he got back to the reason he was there. Planning the event.

"I called Drake Arless. He's free that night. He sent me the menu options. I'll read them to you." Ty pulled up the note on his phone and read her the menu items and their prices. "What do you think?"

"The smoked chicken is a firm yes for me. Should we offer both the pulled pork and the ribs, too?"

"You probably know better than I do."

"Let's go with the ribs, the chicken, mac and cheese, cornbread and slaw." Her satisfied nod brought out her dimples. He couldn't look away from them.

"Okay. I'll let him know." Easy enough. On to the next item... "I'm not sure what to do about the flyers and getting raffle baskets."

"Here's what we used to do..." She explained how she'd been in a sorority and the types of baskets they'd gotten from donors. Then they went back and forth over what to include on the flyers. By the time they were finished, Ty's stomach grumbled.

"Why don't we get a pizza?" he asked, rising to retrieve his phone from his pocket. "Unless you're tired. I can leave."

"Pizza sounds good."

"I'll order it. Any requests?" He found the contact info on his phone for Cowboy John's.

"Pepperoni. No onions."

"Meat lovers?" He glanced her way. Her big blue eyes sparkled as she nodded. He called in the order to have it delivered. "Done."

"Tell me about Jewel River." Ashlinn set the notebook in the basket next to her chair and gave him her full attention. "You grew up here, right?"

"I did." He lowered himself to the couch again. "What do you want to know?"

"Everything."

"That narrows it down." He let out a soft chuckle. "Winters are bitterly cold. Beautiful, though. There's something special about riding out to check cattle when the air's so clear and cold it makes your breath crack. Summers can get real hot. This town lives for festivals—there's a Christmas festival, Easter egg hunt, Fourth of July fest, Labor Day parade, harvest festival. Oh, and Shakespeare-in-the-Park—a movie, not a live performance. It's relatively new."

"I thought Shakespeare-in-the-Park events were for plays." She tucked her legs under her body.

"They are. But not in Jewel River. One of the legacy club members has a grandson in high school who reimagines Shakespeare plays and films them with local actors and props."

"Are they any good?" She scrunched her nose as if she couldn't picture it.

"Honestly? I have no idea. I don't go to them. But I did see the preview for this year's film. I have to admit it was entertaining."

"When is it?"

"August, I think. I can't remember the date. Everyone brings lawn chairs and quilts to the park, and they watch it on a big projector screen."

"Why don't you go?"

He shrugged.

"Are you going to attend it this year?"

He winced. Going would mean talking to the people he'd been avoiding. They all meant well, but… "I don't think so."

"Why not?"

"It's not my thing."

"What is your thing?"

Tough question. Did he even know anymore? "I spend a lot of time at my ranch, riding around the pastures, checking the cattle. It's peaceful out there."

"I'm sure it is." Her wistful expression made him wish she'd come out and see it for herself. But she'd said no—more than once—and he needed to take the hint. "What about the other festivals? What happens at them?"

"Honestly? I don't know."

"You told me all the fun things to do around here, but you don't do any of them?" Her incredulous tone caught him off guard.

Put like that… It wouldn't make sense to anyone else, but it did to him. "I guess not."

"That makes me feel better." Her remark confused him. "Why?"

"Means I'm not the only one staying home." She laughed. How could she have such a good attitude? Ashlinn didn't attend local festivals due to her health. Ty didn't attend them by choice. Something uncomfortable settled in his gut.

Maybe he should change the subject.

"Oh, my mom wants you to join her book club." Why

had that come out of his mouth? "They only read romance novels."

There. He'd warned her.

"How kind of her." She glanced away. "It's not a good time. I'll have to pass."

Disappointment warred with relief. "I don't blame you. Not much of a reader myself."

"I like to read."

"Not romance novels, though."

"I like romance novels."

"Oh."

"It's not the books. I'd be embarrassed if I fainted there. And I have Peanut. He's big. I wouldn't want it to be awkward."

"You clearly don't know my mom. No dog is too big for her house. No amount of fainting would deter her."

"Really?" She seemed genuinely surprised.

"Really."

"I'll keep that in mind."

The doorbell rang and Ty answered the door. After paying for the pizza, he brought it to the dining area. Ashlinn went to the kitchen for plates.

He couldn't remember the last time he'd gone to anyone's house other than Cade's or his mother's. Yet, he felt comfortable at Ashlinn's. She was easy to be with, fun to talk to, and he was glad they were planning the event together. Maybe going to one of those festivals wouldn't be so bad. Should he start taking advantage of what Jewel River had to offer?

Maybe if Ashlinn was by his side.

Chapter Five

Stretched out on the couch with a blanket over her, Ashlinn clicked through television channels. Nothing interested her. What did she expect for a Friday afternoon?

Over two weeks had passed since she and Ty had shared the pizza and discussed the fundraiser. Since then, she'd seen him several times. He dropped by the training center often, and they'd made progress planning for the September event. The flyers were being printed locally and would be ready by the end of next week. She'd been playing around with software to make graphics to share on social media for the event, too.

Unfortunately, every time she got a taste of normal life, she ended up having a health setback. Stomach problems had kept her home for four days. The nausea had been unbearable. The first two days, she hadn't been able to keep much down. Yesterday, she'd turned the corner, but she still felt weak.

Patrick and Mackenzie took turns stopping by each day, and they'd brought her crackers, sports drinks and foods easy to digest. Even Ty's mother, Christy Moulten, had checked on her. She'd also dropped off a romance novel. Ashlinn had thought Ty had been joking about it. She'd been wrong.

Christy was delightful—a force to be reckoned with, for sure—and kind. An older gentleman had driven her, Clem something or other, and scowled at Ashlinn from the driveway where he'd climbed back in his truck rather than come inside. He wasn't someone she expected getting to know very well.

She really should make another cup of tea to stay hydrated.

It took forever to shift her legs over the side of the couch and place her feet on the floor. Were the nausea and vomiting signs her health was regressing? She could *not* become bedridden again. Fear gripped her throat. Had she come this far to only come this far? If the stomach problems persisted, she might be forced to move back home. She shuddered at the thought.

Pushing off the arm of the couch, she stood. Waited for the dizziness to clear. Peanut smelled her hand. "Good boy."

She shuffled to the kitchen and turned on the electric kettle. The stomach problems were temporary—they had to be. Because she wasn't giving up her new life. Helping Patrick's dogs detect her health issues gave her purpose. And she enjoyed typing his clients' information into spreadsheets.

She'd finally gotten a taste of feeling useful. Would her sense of value be snatched away along with her independence?

A knock at the front door startled her.

It was too early for Patrick or Mackenzie to stop by, and she wasn't expecting any packages. With a sigh, she slowly padded to the front door. Ty and Fritz stood on the welcome mat.

"Why are you here?" She opened the door wide, not caring her hair was a mess and she still wore the T-shirt and shorts she'd slept in last night. Peanut wagged his tail next to her, and Fritz lifted his nose to greet him.

"Heard you were under the weather. I brought soup." He held up a plastic bag. "Can I come in?"

"Sure. Don't mind me, though. I know I'm a wreck."

"You could never be a wreck."

Did he not have eyes? He brushed past her, and she closed

the door and followed him to the kitchen. After he took off Fritz's leash, the dogs greeted each other in circles, then Peanut came over. He didn't alert her, thankfully.

"I hope you like chicken noodle." He set the bag on the counter and lifted out plastic containers. Cracked the lid off one.

"I love chicken noodle. I don't know how much I'll be able to eat, though. Still working through some stomach issues. Don't worry—I'm not contagious. I'm just dealing with a flare-up." She saw no point in pretending otherwise.

"If you can't eat it today, it'll be good for a few days in the fridge. Want a bowl now?" The aroma of chicken broth filled the air. She almost declined, but the smell made her hungry.

"A small bowl. And please, help yourself to one, too." A wave of exhaustion overcame her, and she padded to the dining table. Pulled out a chair and sat, resting her elbow on the table with her cheek against her palm. Much better.

"I'll have a biscuit and leave the soup for you." He ladled soup into a bowl and arranged biscuits around a small mound of butter on a plate. Then he set the bowl in front of her. "One sec. I'll get you a spoon."

How she longed to tell him she'd do it herself, but her weary body refused to cooperate. All she could do was sit there, thankful for his help. Fritz trotted over and sat next to her chair. He looked up with big eyes. How could anyone not pet the little darling? She stroked his back.

"It's good to see you, Fritz." Feeling off, she didn't have the energy to bring her hand back up. Fritz nudged her hand with his nose, just like Peanut would. In fact, Peanut came over and stared. Uh-oh. An episode was on the way.

How could standing, opening the door and walking to the kitchen make her feel like she'd run a marathon? Peanut must not be too concerned, though. He left to find Ty with his tail wagging.

"Here you go." Ty placed a spoon and butter knife next to her bowl, then took a seat to her left and reached for a biscuit. He tore one open and slathered it with butter before taking a bite.

She dipped the spoon into the soup and discreetly checked him out. His dark brown eyes and cropped black hair accentuated his tanned face. He'd taken off his straw cowboy hat and wore a dark T-shirt that stretched across his muscles. Although the temperature outside was hot, he was in jeans and cowboy boots. She doubted she'd ever see him in anything else. Wouldn't bother her a bit. He looked good in them.

"Do you need me to take you to the doctor?"

"I'm doing okay. I know the signs of dehydration. I'm not there yet." She turned her attention to the soup and lifted a small bite to her lips. "Mmm. This is good."

"Glad you like it. I've been perfecting the recipe for the past couple of years."

"You made this?" The soup tasted like health in a bowl. The perfect ratio of chicken, vegetables, noodles and broth.

"I did."

The cowboy continued to surprise her. She took another spoonful. The warm broth went down easy.

"Want a biscuit?" He held up the plate.

"I'd better not. The soup isn't bothering me. I'd be pushing it if I tried anything else."

He nodded, and she appreciated that he accepted her answer. Her mother would have gotten increasingly agitated, insisting she try a bite. And Ashlinn would have hated the shrillness in her tone, eventually caving, only to get sick again.

"If you need anything, you can call or text me anytime." Sincerity oozed from him. Hearing those kind words relieved something deep inside her—the awful feeling of being a burden. Her parents weren't perfect, but they'd never made her feel like one.

"Thank you." It would be so nice to have him on speed dial. Relying on people other than her family was new to her. She wouldn't take advantage of him.

Neither spoke as they continued to eat.

"I hear my mom and Clem stopped by." Ty's amused eyes caught her off guard. He looked younger when he wasn't so serious.

"They did. Clem stayed in the driveway, glaring at me. Is he a serial killer or something?"

Ty barked out a laugh. "Serial killer? No. That's just Clem being Clem. He's actually a good guy."

"If you say so."

"He's brutally honest. Tells it like it is. He and my mom go round and round arguing whenever they're together."

"Are they together a lot? Like a couple?"

"No—oh, no. My mom's driver's license is constantly being revoked. She's a terrible driver. Ever since she moved from the ranch to her house in town, Clem has taken it upon himself to be her driver. I think it keeps them both out of trouble."

"Did she live on your ranch?"

"Actually, she lived on the ranch where I grew up. Cade owns it now. Before our father died, he divided the property. Dad owned a lot of acreage, and it made sense for us to each have our own operations."

"Have you ever lived anywhere else?"

"No. Jewel River is home. Cade lived in New York City for several years, though. He moved back for good after our father died."

"You're close to your brother, aren't you?" She nudged the bowl away.

"Yeah, I am."

"Your mom gave me a romance novel. Told me to keep the first Thursday of the month open for book club."

"What did I tell you? That's my mom. Always trying to get people to join her book club. Are you thinking of going?"

"No," she said with a self-deprecating shrug. "I told her I don't drive, and she said you would drop me off. I wouldn't want you to do that. I told her it would be too complicated with Peanut and my fainting."

"I'm sure she had a reply for that," he muttered.

"She told me she's used to being around service dogs since she trained Tulip. And she assured me I would have a comfy chair in case I fainted."

"Mom doesn't know how to take no for an answer."

Ashlinn privately agreed. "Then she said no one would even notice if I fainted, since a few of the older members fall asleep on occasion—apparently, I'd fit right in."

His expression blanked. "She didn't."

"She did." Ashlinn's lips twitched. At the time she'd been surprised, but looking back, it was kind of funny.

"I'm sorry. I don't know what to say. She's—"

"Wonderful. Your mom is wonderful." Ashlinn meant it. "But I still told her no."

"Good. You need to do what's right for you." He glanced toward the back door. "The weather's nice. Have you been able to get outside much?"

"No. I haven't been feeling good. I've been in bed or on the couch."

"Why don't we go out back? It's a beautiful day. I'll set up a lawn chair for you."

"I don't have a lawn chair." If she did, though…she wouldn't mind sitting out there in the sunshine.

"You do now." He stood and grinned. "I'll be right back."

What was he talking about? He went to the back door. She wanted to rush over to the window to watch him, but she'd better conserve the little energy she had. Her top priority at the moment was making herself presentable.

She went to her bedroom and changed into a clean shirt and shorts. Peanut followed her. Then she crossed the hall to the bathroom and brushed her hair. She returned to the kitchen. Ty opened the back door and offered her his arm. She was thankful for his strong muscles to lean on as they carefully made their way down the steps. Two loungers and two Adirondack chairs were set up on the lawn. Side tables had been placed between them.

She blinked back tears. "It's like a tropical oasis in my backyard."

Peanut was nosing around all the furniture. With his nose to the ground, too, Fritz trotted around the perimeter of the fence, then came over to them in leaps and bounds. Peanut looked up at them with his tongue hanging out.

"See? Even the dogs approve." Ty helped her sit on one of the loungers, and as she stretched out her legs, she heaved a sigh of relief. He was right. The sun felt amazing.

"How much do I owe you for the chairs?" She glanced over at Ty, who'd taken a seat in the lounger next to her with a content expression on his face.

"Nothing."

"I have to pay you."

"No, you don't. You didn't ask for them. And I had an ulterior motive."

"Ulterior motive, huh?" She wasn't buying it. He kept doing nice things for her, and what did she give him in return? Not a whole lot.

"Yes. I was thinking about buying a set of loungers like this for my place. Now I know they're comfortable."

"Then take these with you." She didn't want to be in his debt. And she couldn't really afford the chairs.

"Nope. I got a deal on a four-pack. Two for you, and two for me." He wiggled his shoulders and closed his eyes with his hands on his washboard abs. "I'm going to string some patio lights over there, too, if you don't object."

"Really?" She could picture lights strung overhead, like the ones she secretly wanted whenever she scrolled through her phone. This man was so thoughtful.

"Yes, really. I wouldn't lie about it."

"Thank you. That's so generous and thoughtful of you." The sound of birds chirping and the wind gently rustling the leaves in the nearby tree were more relaxing than any music could be. Within moments, drowsiness overtook her.

She must have fallen asleep because when she woke, she sensed that if she tried to get up, she'd pass out. Peanut had noticed, too, because he was sitting next to her chair, staring at her. He began licking her hand. She petted him. "Good boy. Good boy."

"What do you need?" Ty shifted to face her, placing his feet on the ground between their chairs.

"Potato chips. Water." She didn't bother insisting on getting them herself. Her blood pressure was low, and she needed the salt and the fluids. Could kick herself for not bringing them out here. Too in a rush to enjoy the weather. Too excited to be with Ty. She made a mental note to prepare better if she came outside alone.

"Done."

A few minutes later, he handed her a bag of potato chips and her tumbler full of ice water. She thanked him and munched on a few chips.

"You okay?"

She nodded. "It's funny, but I never thought I'd be able to do this with someone other than my parents."

"What do you mean?" He'd shifted to recline on the lounger again but kept his head turned to watch her.

"I don't know." She took a long drink. Nice and cold. "I guess I didn't think I'd feel comfortable having anyone see me like this."

"Getting a suntan?" he teased.

"Ha ha." She threw a potato chip at him. He caught it and grinned. She grinned back. "You're seeing my normal life. Bedhead, weak, on the verge of passing out. It's not something many people have witnessed, and surprisingly, it's not as humiliating as I'd worried it would be."

"Good. It shouldn't be." He popped the chip into his mouth. "Toss me another, would you?"

She handed him the bag, and he took a handful before passing it back.

"What about your friends?" he asked. "You know, before you moved here?"

That brought a pang to her chest. She didn't have the best track record with friends. "They all kind of moved on with their lives. I didn't have a best friend in high school. I hung out with a group of girls, and after graduating, we all went our separate ways. None of my college friends lived nearby, and the ones who made an effort quit coming around after years of me not being able to go anywhere."

He probably thought she was a loser for not having friends.

"I pushed my friends away." His gruff words were not what she was expecting. "They refused to give up on me, though. My brother made it his mission to barge into my life whenever he feels like it. Mom, too. I used to resent it."

"You don't anymore?"

He shook his head, wiping the crumbs from his hands. "I

don't. He loves me. Worries about me. And I can honestly say if our roles were reversed, I'd do the same to him."

"He seems nice. He's stopped by the center with Mackenzie a few times. What about the rest of your friends?"

"A couple of guys moved back recently—Dean McCaffrey, he's a builder here in town if you need any work done, and Trent Lloyd, who manages Cade's horse-boarding business. I should drive you over there sometime. I think you'd like the stables."

At that, she directed her attention to the tumbler in her hand. Ty seemed to keep forgetting she couldn't go wherever she pleased. He'd asked her out to his ranch, and now he wanted her to see his brother's stables?

He didn't get it.

For the past four days, she'd barely been able to stand. How could she possibly leave her house and drive somewhere with him?

She couldn't. And she needed to keep that in mind before she went all gaga over the cowboy sitting next to her.

Still…until yesterday she hadn't even considered spending time in her backyard. Maybe because there wasn't any patio furniture. No safe spot for her to lie down if her blood pressure dropped.

Ty had made this possible. And if he could give her a safe space in her yard, what else could he do?

How many of her *I can'ts* were real, and how many were simply fears?

An hour later, Ty knocked on his mom's front door. Figured he'd try to be a better son and make more of an effort with her. She'd never given up on him, and he'd provided her plenty of reasons to in the past couple of years. Gratitude—

especially for how she'd reached out to Ashlinn to make her feel welcome—flooded him. His mom was special.

Ashlinn had barely been able to keep her eyes open when he'd taken off. First, he'd made her promise she'd call or text him if she needed anything. He'd also told her he'd be back in the morning with doughnuts from Annie's Bakery. She hadn't seemed enthused about it. Doughnuts might not have been the best suggestion since she was sick. Or was her lack of enthusiasm due to him coming over again?

They'd clicked all afternoon. She'd said she felt comfortable with him, and he felt the same. It hadn't bothered him that she was tired and low on energy. In fact, he'd liked helping her, liked the way her face had lit up when he'd shown her the outdoor furniture. He'd enjoyed their teasing banter. The woman had no idea how beautiful she was, bedhead and all.

"I wasn't expecting you!" His mom's mouth spread into a smile full of wonder. She pulled him in for a hug. "Charlene's here, and Clem's coming over in a bit—we figured the fish fry at Dixie B's was the right move. You'll join us, of course. Four is better than three."

"Char's here?" He retreated a step, but Fritz surged forward at the sight of Tulip, his mother's Pomeranian. "I'll come back another time."

"Yoo-hoo, Ty!" Charlene Parker called from the living room. "Get your cute self in here and give me a hug."

He winced, shifting his jaw. Just one of the reasons he didn't drop by his mother's house very often. There was no telling who'd be visiting. Charlene and his mother together unsettled him. He knew exactly what he was walking into— the latest gossip, endless questions about the fundraiser and not so subtle hints about dating Ashlinn.

These two had been trying to set him up with every single woman in his age range for years. Ew.

His mom took him by the arm and practically dragged him inside. The dogs finished greeting each other, and Ty bent to pet fluffy Tulip. Then he went over to Charlene.

"Hi, Charlene." He gave her a hug and sat at the other end of the couch. She was the director of the small nursing home where his grandmother lived. "How's everything at the nursing home?"

"Good as it can be, hon." She picked up a dainty teacup and took a sip. "Miss Trudy's been sleeping more lately."

Trudy Moulten, his paternal grandmother, had been living at the home for a few years. Her Alzheimer's was getting worse. His mother brought Tulip to see her almost every day. "Is that good or bad?"

"A bit of both. She's confused a lot, so sleeping gives her peace." Charlene's affectionate tone eased his worries. "Now, where is little Fritz?"

Good question. He looked around. "He should be here—oh, there he is." The mini-doxie trotted to Charlene's feet, waiting for her to pick him up. She promptly snuggled the dog to her chest. He gave her cheek a lick, and she laughed. "Sweet Fritzie."

"Did you check on Ashlinn?" Mom settled into an overstuffed chair and propped her feet on the ottoman. "I like her. I might have convinced her to join the book club. I hope she's feeling better soon."

"Stomach bug?" Charlene continued to pet Fritz, who'd taken the opportunity to sit on her lap. The dog seemed to know he'd be pampered there.

"She called it a flare-up," Ty said. "She looked pale. The weakness is due to her autoimmune disease."

"Poor thing." His mom shook her head, making a tsking noise. "So pretty and so young. Doesn't seem fair her life is so limited due to her health."

"At least she's alive." Ty hadn't meant to sound bitter. But it occurred to him that Zoey's life had been limited, too, but she'd died. She'd never have a chance to enjoy afternoons in the backyard anymore.

"True, but I wish she had her health," his mom said. "From what I understand, she's nearly homebound when it comes to activities. It's got to be hard."

"She doesn't see it that way." He propped an ankle on the opposite knee.

"How *does* she see it?" Charlene mindlessly petted Fritz.

He squirmed a little. Why hadn't he kept his mouth shut? Let them do all the talking as usual? They were good at it. Better than he was.

"I gather she's glad to have some freedom again."

"Freedom?" Charlene gave his mom a skeptical glance. "If you say so. We haven't seen her around town at all."

"I do say so." It annoyed him that they weren't giving Ashlinn her due. Fritz stepped off Charlene's lap and came over to his. As the dog licked his forearm, Ty's tension faded slightly. "She's spent the past six years relying on her parents for everything. And now she's living in a house on her own, and she even has a part-time job. Both were more than she could have hoped for previously."

"You're right." Charlene had a contrite air. "I guess it depends on how you look at things."

"I, for one, hope we all see a lot more of her. I gave her this month's book since *someone* was being a baby and refused to give it to her." Mom gave him serious side-eye.

"I'm not carrying around a book with a dude holding twin babies on the cover."

"What if the man was a cowboy and there were no babies?" Mom asked. "Would you take her a book if it had mountains on it or something?"

"No." He had to be firm. If he agreed to one cowboy or mountains, she'd start pressuring him to deliver books with babies and dogs and guys making googly eyes at some woman. Wasn't happening.

The women exchanged disappointed stares. He willed himself not to squirm.

"It's just a book," Mom said. "I'm not asking for much."

"Why are you mad?" He opened his hands. "The book club is your pride and joy, not mine. I'm not doing your dirty work."

"Dirty work." His mother shook her head as if he'd lost his mind. "I'm asking you to drop off a novel, Ty, not smuggle drugs."

He knew better than to respond.

"So where are you at with the event planning?" Charlene took another sip of tea.

He filled them in on everything, including the flyers and social media graphics Ashlinn had made.

"Did you figure out what you're doing about the silent auction yet?" Mom asked.

"No. I'll ask Ashlinn about it when she's feeling better."

"Why don't you let us handle it?" Her face lit up. "We can go around town and ask for donations. I stop by most of the businesses every week, anyhow."

He opened his mouth to decline her offer, but then he closed it. His mother and Charlene were perfect for the job. They knew everyone in Jewel River and had no problem asking for donations.

"Actually, that would be a big help, Mom."

She blinked a few times. He braced himself for...something.

"You're letting me help?" Her voice sounded strangled, and her eyes shimmered in surprise.

"Yeah. You'll be great at it. Better than me."

She pushed Tulip off her lap, stood and crossed over to him. He rose slightly as she hugged him. Then she kissed his right cheek and nodded, clearly emotional.

What was that all about?

"This is the first time you've accepted an offer of help from me in years."

She was right, and he hadn't realized his dismissal had hurt her. "I'm sorry—"

"No, no. I didn't mention it to make you feel bad. Something's changed with you, Ty, and I like it. I hope you'll continue letting me help."

He ran his finger along the collar of his T-shirt. "Um, sure."

A knock on the door sent his mother in motion. "That must be Clem. Ty, will Fritz be okay here alone with Tulip?"

"I'm not going out to eat."

"Yes, you are," she said on her way to the door. "Look at them." Fritz had jumped up on her chair and smooshed in next to Tulip. "Fritzie will be fine here."

"Come on." Clem's gruff voice filled the room. "We need to leave now if we want to get a table."

Ty waited for Charlene to gather her purse, then followed her to the door, where Clem's eyes widened in surprise. "Christy didn't tell me you were here. Finally. A man. These two hens will be clucking nonstop. I might be able to eat in peace."

"We are *not* chickens, Clem." His mom hiked her purse strap over her shoulder and marched down the porch steps to his truck. "And we don't cluck."

Clem strode after her. "You two gab so much no one can get a word in."

"Oh, and you're such a talker."

Ty closed the door and followed them to the driveway. His

mom waited for Clem to open the back door for her. Ty jogged around the other side and held open the door for Charlene.

Once the women were settled, he gave them a nod. "I'm going home."

"Don't be a ninny." Clem climbed into the truck. "Get in. Time's a wasting."

"Maybe next time."

"Get. In." Clem's steely eyes meant business.

Ty sighed.

"What? You think there's a rattlesnake on the seat, boy?" Clem made a sucking sound with his teeth.

Ty climbed into the passenger seat. Clem backed out of the drive.

"Clem, you'd be bored out of your mind without us around," Charlene said. "We keep things lively."

"Bored? I don't think so."

Panic set in as Ty realized he was voluntarily going to Dixie B's with his mother, her best friend and Clem.

He didn't go out to dinner with people. Not even his family.

Maybe his mother was right. Something *had* changed. He wasn't sure he was ready for this new development.

What would it hurt? His mom and Charlene would do all the talking. And Clem would glower at anyone who stopped by to say hello. Dining with these three was probably the best-case scenario if he ever wanted to start getting out and about town more often. But did he want to? It was too late to back out now.

Chapter Six

The man had brought doughnuts, and Ashlinn loved a good pastry.

"I've got crullers, cinnamon rolls, long johns, pumpkin doughnuts—you name it. I hope you don't mind. I know you haven't been feeling great." Ty lifted the lid off the box marked Annie's Bakery in her kitchen the next morning. She'd been ready when he'd arrived a few minutes past ten. She'd even showered and done her hair. Yesterday, both had been impossible.

"Ooh, the cinnamon roll, please." She set two small plates on the counter. Then she straightened the red-and-white checked dish towel hanging from the oven handle. "Want a cup of coffee?"

"Sure." Icing from the cinnamon roll oozed on one plate, and a cruller and pumpkin doughnut were crammed on the other. Sunlight streamed in through the window over the sink. He pointed to the coffeepot. "I can pour if you'd like to sit and rest."

"I'm okay." She took out two mugs from an upper cabinet. "I think the fresh air and soup yesterday helped me turn the corner. I feel much better."

"I'm glad to hear it."

"I have flavored cream in the fridge if you want it."

"No thanks. I take my coffee black."

She poured the coffee and brought the mugs to the table where Ty had carried the plates. Peanut glued himself to her side and licked his doggy lips twice.

"You're not getting any of this, mister." She stroked Peanut's soft, furry head.

"What are you doing today?" Ty sat in the same chair he had yesterday. "Do you need a hand with anything?"

She'd known him less than a month, and he'd continued to go out of his way to help her. She tore off a small chunk of the roll and popped it in her mouth. After chewing, she stared at him. "Actually, I wanted to ask you something."

"What?"

"I've thought about it, and I'd like to see your ranch." Her nerves jittered over what could happen, but excitement rose, too. The more she'd thought about it last night, the more she realized she wanted to expand her world. Little by little. Inch by inch.

"When?" He toyed with the handle of the mug.

"Today?" She cringed a bit. Was she ready? "I'd need to bring supplies. And I might not be able to do much besides sit."

"You want to visit my ranch?" An incredulous grin spread across his face. "Today?"

She nodded. Why was he so happy about it? It wasn't like she could ride horses or rope cows or whatever people did on ranches.

"I don't want you to be nervous." He extended his arm, palm out. "We'll sit on my front porch. I've got a pair of rocking chairs. We'll watch the world go by. It's my favorite thing to do."

A rush of emotion had her blinking away tears. Rocking

on a front porch sounded absolutely wonderful. Could he truly want something so simple?

"Good, because that's about all I can do right now," she said. "I don't want you to be disappointed."

"Never." He pushed his chair back and stood. "What do we need to bring?"

She laughed, pointing for him to sit again. "Let's enjoy our coffee first."

He gave her a sheepish grin.

"What did you do last night?" she asked, sipping her coffee.

"Believe it or not, I went out to supper with my mom, her best friend and Clem."

"Why would that be hard to believe?" She assumed he dined with them often.

"I don't go out to eat very often."

"No?"

"I don't get out much in general." He bit into the cruller.

"Why not?"

"After Zoey died, it was too hard."

Zoey. Again. Ashlinn tried not to let the name bother her. She'd ignore the sudden burst of heartburn it produced.

"Is it still hard?" she asked.

"More uncomfortable than hard, I guess."

"Six years, right? Maybe being alone became a habit."

"Maybe." He didn't meet her eyes.

Another thought occurred. "Do you think you've been depressed?"

When he didn't immediately say no, she took it as a yes.

"What's changed?" She lifted her mug to take a sip.

"Nothing." Then he rubbed his chin. "A lot of things."

"Like what?"

"My brother marrying Mackenzie. Mom moving to town.

Patrick opening the center. My buddies settling here again. I guess I started to wake up to the world around me."

"I'm glad you did." His honesty touched her.

"Why?"

"Otherwise, you wouldn't have adopted Fritz, and we probably wouldn't have met."

"I think you're right." His thoughtful expression was tinged with sadness. "I wouldn't have wanted to meet you."

Ouch. That comment stung.

"But I would have missed out." His searing gaze and tender tone chased away the sting. "I'm glad we met."

"I am, too." She polished off half of her cinnamon roll and stood. "Let me get a few things together, and we can go."

"What do you need? Let me help."

"The weighted blanket folded next to the couch. I'll grab my blood pressure monitor."

"Don't forget the chips and water." He headed to the living room.

"I won't." Her phone rang on the way to her bedroom. She answered it. "Hey, Mom, what's up?"

"How are you doing? Have you eaten anything? I called the clinic in Jewel River, and they can give you an IV on Monday when they open."

Ashlinn slowed, her good mood crashing. "I'm doing okay. I'm eating again. Yesterday was much better than the rest of the week."

"Can you call Patrick to take you to the doctor on Monday for the IV?" Her voice was shrill.

"It's not necessary."

"Not necessary? The last time you had stomach problems, you were in bed for a week."

"And this time I bounced back more quickly." She suppressed her mounting frustration. "In fact, I feel good enough to go on a small adventure today."

"Adventure? Absolutely not. Please don't tell me you're walking to work."

"It's Saturday. The center's closed." She forced herself to the bedroom, where she located the monitor and grabbed a hoodie in case it got cold.

"What are you doing, then?"

"Ty is taking me to his ranch." She braced herself for a lecture.

"A ranch?" The long pause didn't help her nerves. "What are you thinking? You can't ride horses. What if you faint? How far away is this place?"

Disappointment seeped to her toes. Her mom never gave her any credit. Always saw the downside. "I didn't say I was riding horses."

"This is going to send you right back to a life in bed. Have you forgotten those days?"

"No, Mom. I haven't forgotten. I know what I'm doing."

"I don't think you do. You're playing games with your health, and who will be around to take care of you when it falls apart this time?"

Why did there have to be a "this time?" Ashlinn gripped the phone tightly. "I'm not talking to you when you're in this mood."

"What mood?" Her mom's voice rose. "I don't know what you're talking about."

"Goodbye." She ended the call and perched on the edge of her bed. Her hands were trembling. Was her mom right? Was she playing games with her health? Would she be bed-ridden if she overdid it by going to the ranch? Her doctors encouraged her to get out if she felt up to it.

"Ashlinn?" Ty called from the living room. She stood and

carried the monitor and hoodie down the hallway, where Ty held up the tote. "Oh, there you are. I've got the blanket, chips and water. Do you need anything else?"

"Peanut." She tried to smile, but she was pretty sure her face was cracking.

"Hey, are you okay?" He put his hand on her shoulder, and she almost burst into tears. "If you're not feeling good—"

"I feel good." She lifted her chin and looked into his eyes. "Let's get out of here."

Questions lingered in his eyes, but he gave her a nod. She helped Peanut into his vest. Took a deep breath.

God, I don't know if this is the right decision or not, but I know You'll be with me today, and that's all I really need.

Ty held the door open, and she and the dog headed outside. Something told her she had nothing to worry about as long as Ty was at her side. A taste of life—an afternoon somewhere new—was exactly what she needed. And if her health fell apart? Her mom could tell her, "I told you so."

"Wait right there." Ty got out of the truck and jogged around the front to open the passenger door for Ashlinn. She'd been quiet during the half-hour ride. He'd turned the radio to a country station and watched the world go by. When she'd told him she wanted to see his ranch, he'd been shocked—and excited. And in his haste to make it happen, he'd overlooked one important question. Could he handle it if anything went wrong?

What if she had a medical emergency? His ranch was thirty minutes from town, and the nearest hospital was a good hour and a half away.

Ashlinn might look fine, but she was still recovering from her flare-up. He should have told her they could come out next weekend. But he hadn't. Selfishly, he'd wanted to bring her here today. Probably because he feared she'd change her mind in a week.

Being around Ashlinn made him feel alive. And he hadn't felt alive in a long time.

"Are you ready for this?" He took her hand and helped her climb out. Then he let Peanut out of the backseat. The dog always appeared to be smiling. Ty grabbed the tote from the floor and offered Ashlinn his arm. Together, they strolled to his front porch. He ignored the way his heartbeat pounded at the feel of her small hand in the crook of his arm.

"Wow, Ty." She turned to him. "All this is yours?"

His chest expanded. He was proud of his home and property. "Yes. The house, outbuildings, corrals, pastures—all of it. My land stops at those trees." He pointed to a forest in the far distance. "Come on. I'll show you around inside."

The front door led directly into his living room. Hardwood floors, dark brown furniture and white walls—suited him just fine. The place had never had a woman's touch.

"It's lovely." She let go of his arm and drifted over to the picture window. "I can't get over your view." Beyond the lawn, the prairie rolled out for miles.

"I could stare at it all day." Although, at the moment, the only thing he was staring at was her.

"Me, too." She turned to him with a soft smile, and he couldn't help wondering what it would be like to kiss her. *Slow down, cowboy. You're not kissing anyone.*

"I'll, uh, set everything right here." He put her tote next to the coffee table on the rug. "Can I get you something to drink?"

"No, I'm fine. Oh, there you are, Fritz." Fritz bypassed Ty to run straight to her, and she bent to pet him. Ty didn't blame the dog. He was drawn to her, too.

When she straightened, she thrust her hand out to steady

herself, but all it met with was air. She began to sway. Peanut hurried over, and Ty sprang into action, putting his arm around her waist.

"Whoa, there. You okay?" He guided her to the couch and helped her sit. Peanut stayed by her side, staring at her. "Do you want to lie down?"

"I'd better sit on the floor. I could faint and fall off the couch. I try to stay on the ground when Peanut alerts me. Could you put a pillow and the weighted blanket down there?" She pointed to the area rug. "I'll drink some water. Maybe this will pass."

"Do you feel like you're going to faint?" He brought over her weighted blanket and set a throw pillow on the rug. Peanut put his paw on the blanket.

"Peanut wants me on the floor. When he acts like this, I usually pass out within minutes. See how he's focused on the blanket? He wants me down there." She scooted forward, and Ty assisted her to the floor. Peanut lay next to her, licking her hand. Fritz bounced over and tried to sit on her lap, but Ty scooped up the mutt and cradled him to his chest.

"Leave Ashlinn alone. She's not feeling good, buddy." The dog licked his chin and wiggled to get down. Ty set him on all fours but commanded him to sit. Fritz obeyed. Anxiety began rising within him.

"I need the blood pressure cuff." Her voice faded.

"I'll get it." He set her tumbler of water next to her and rooted through the tote to find the blood pressure monitor. His fingers shook as he carried it over.

"Thanks." She stretched out her legs and placed the weighted blanket over her shins. Peanut sat upright next to her. She wrapped her arm around him. "You know it's coming, don't you, boy?"

"Want me to put this on?" Ty held up the cuff, hating how helpless he felt.

"Cover." Her voice grew weaker as she pointed to her lap. Panting, Peanut draped his body over her thighs. "Good boy."

"Ashlinn?" Ty's nerves frayed. What should he do? Fritz came over and whined. Ashlinn's breathing grew shallow and her eyes closed as she stroked Peanut's fur. The dog licked her forearm and hand.

"Cuff." Without opening her eyes, she touched her left wrist. He ripped the Velcro and wrapped the cuff around it. Then he pressed the start button. Peanut continued licking her hand, and she kept praising him. She shifted from sitting to lying on the rug with her head on the pillow.

Ty knelt beside her with no clue what to do. On her other side, Peanut licked and nibbled her fingers and wrist.

She'd passed out. Her arm was limp. She was unresponsive.

Fear spread through his core. Peanut wouldn't stop licking her arm, and Fritz came over, clearly aware something was happening, and put his front paws on Ty's thighs.

Should he check her blood pressure? Shake her?

What if she didn't wake up?

Get yourself together. Fritz licked his hand. Great. The dog was copying Peanut, and Ty was pretty sure he wasn't the one with the medical problems.

He checked the monitor on her wrist. Her blood pressure was low. Too low. Another wave of anxiety crested. Fritz licked his hand again, and he picked up the dog, hugging him to his chest. He began to feel calmer.

"Good boy," she whispered.

Ty inhaled sharply. She was conscious! *Thank You, Lord. Thank You!*

Peanut no longer licked her hand. Instead, he softly panted

and stayed beside her. She opened her eyes and closed them again. A few moments later, she moved her arms slightly. Peanut licked her fingers again. Her face was pale. She looked exhausted.

As Ty sat there watching her, he was thankful for Fritz's warm body in his arms.

What seemed like a lifetime later but was probably only a few minutes, Ashlinn turned her head and stared at him through unfocused eyes. "I'm okay."

She didn't sound okay.

"Stay where you are, Ash. Can I get you anything? Do anything?"

"Legs." Her hand flopped as she pointed to her lower legs.

He moved the weighted blanket, not sure what she was asking him to do. Then she made a scrunching motion with her fingers. He set Fritz on the floor and gently massaged her lower legs. Fritz joined Peanut, sniffing Ashlinn's arm. Ty continued to compress her calves, grateful to be doing something—anything—to take his mind off his helplessness.

"Almost there." She turned her head. "Thank you."

He nodded, touched by her gratitude. He'd done next to nothing. Wished he could have prevented it. She reached for her tumbler of water, and he put it in her hand. "Can I help you sit up?"

"Not yet. Give me a few minutes."

"Sure." Peanut ambled away with Fritz. Either the dog wasn't concerned or he was distracted by the wiener dog. Something told him Peanut wasn't easily distracted.

True to her word, Ashlinn shifted to her side and dragged the weighted blanket over her legs once more. Peanut was off doing his own thing, and Fritz came over wagging his tail. She caressed the little dog. "You're worried about me, aren't you?"

"He's not the only one."

She met his gaze, understanding emanating from her eyes. "I know. It's not easy watching me have an episode."

"How long are you usually out?"

Resting her cheek on her arm, she frowned. "It depends. Sometimes only a few seconds. Sometimes longer. If Peanut was still here licking me, I'd probably pass out again, but he's moved on with his life."

"Should he have moved on?" He wanted to know more about what to expect.

"Yes." She looked cute lying there on her side with her cheek on her upper arm and her blond hair spilling out across the rug. "It means my body's returning to normal. Speaking of which, I'd better check the monitor again."

After reading the number, she began to sit up. She scooted so her back was against the couch. Ty found the bag of potato chips. As soon as he gave it to her, he went to the kitchen, braced his palms against the counter, and let his head drop.

Witnessing a full-blown faint had scared him more than he wanted to admit. Lifting his head, he clenched his jaw. Maybe he shouldn't have asked her to come. Had the drive caused her to faint?

What if she hadn't woken up? What would he have done then?

He had to stop that line of thinking. She *had* recovered. She'd been able to prepare for it. She'd known what to do, and Peanut had, too.

After centering himself, he returned to the living room and fount Ashlinn attempting to stand. He rushed over and helped her sit on the couch.

"Thank you." She crunched on a chip. "Regret inviting me yet?" Her tone was teasing, but worry ran deep within her eyes.

"Of course not." He wanted her there. He just didn't want to make her sick. Wished she could enjoy it. "I'm glad you're here."

"Me, too." She ate another chip.

"I wasn't sure what to do. What if you didn't wake up?" He hoped she wouldn't be offended by his question.

"I always wake up. That's one thing you don't have to worry about. The danger is when I'm not able to get to a safe position before fainting. I could fall and hit my head—that sort of thing."

An image of her on the ground with a pool of blood spreading through her hair made him pace. Fritz came over and let out a yip. He stared down at the dog.

"He knows when you're nervous." Ashlinn continued eating chips.

"What do you mean?"

"He's alerting you."

"What?" Was it possible?

She nodded, finishing her bite. "He was trained to alert his previous owner, a veteran with anxiety and depression. He's good at picking up on moods."

Huh. Ty hadn't put two and two together. Ashlinn could be right. Fritz always zoomed over when he was stressed. Licked his hand. Demanded attention. Even yipped on occasion.

"I never thought I'd be getting alerted by a service dog." He let out a soft snort, looking at the tiny dog through new eyes.

"Now you know." She took a long drink of water. "I'm feeling much better. And I believe you promised me a rocking chair on the front porch."

"I did." He offered her his hand. Her small fingers felt delicate in his, strengthening his desire to protect her. "You're sure you want to go outside?"

"I'm sure."

"The dogs should be okay out there with us." They made their way to the door. "Or do you think they need leashes?"

"Peanut never strays far from me."

"Fritz doesn't like to be more than ten feet from me." His worries began to fade. "He's always by my side."

Out on the porch, Ty helped her into a rocking chair. Peanut and Fritz jogged down the steps and played with each other on the front lawn. Then Ty went back inside to get her water, the weighted blanket and the blood pressure cuff. Just in case.

The serenity on her face as she rocked and took in the view stole his breath. He'd never have guessed she'd spent the past fifteen minutes dealing with a fainting spell and its aftermath.

"It's beautiful out here, Ty." She sighed in contentment. "I saw a hawk flying overhead."

"You'll see a lot of them." He set everything beside her on the porch, then lowered his frame into the other rocking chair. "In the evenings, you'll see pronghorns and deer."

"This is like something out of a picture book. I'm not used to having such a wide-open view. No neighbors. No houses. Just all this glorious land."

"I feel the same." Except the things she listed could be a liability, too—not for him—but for her.

What happened if she was all alone out here and fainted? Hit her head and was hurt?

"Is it only you running this place?" she asked. Peanut checked on her, then he and Fritz sprawled out on the porch.

"No, I have a full-time ranch hand and a part-timer, too."

"Tell me about what you do here. How does your day begin?"

"Mornings start before dawn. We take care of the horses,

in the winter we feed the cattle…" He gave her an overview of his life as a rancher, answering each question that came up.

"I'd take you on a tour—"

Her laugh cut him off. "No, I don't want to chance it. Right here is perfect."

He gave her a searching stare, then turned his attention to the land before him. Right here was perfect for him, too. Always had been. The fact she felt the same filled him with satisfaction.

And then he remembered Zoey.

Zoey had been the one to suggest he buy two rocking chairs so they'd be able to enjoy the good weather "like a couple of old folks." But she'd died before she could enjoy sitting out there with him.

What would she think of him out here with another woman in her chair?

He stood abruptly. "I'll be right back."

He hurried into the house and marched straight to the bathroom. Splashed water on his face and glanced up at his reflection in the mirror. What was he doing?

Ashlinn wasn't supposed to be part of his life. No woman was.

But he couldn't pretend he wasn't drawn to her. And he'd better get back out there in case she had another fainting spell.

Lighting matches around dry tinder. That was what he was doing. And he'd be the one getting torched if he didn't start guarding his heart.

Chapter Seven

❧

"You should come with us to the Shakespeare-in-the-Park movie." Mackenzie Moulten sat across from Ashlinn at the desk in Patrick's office on Thursday afternoon. Peanut was grooming himself on the dog bed in the corner. Mackenzie had arrived twenty minutes ago telling Ashlinn all about the various ranches she'd been to for herd health visits over the past couple of weeks. Her mobile vet trailer allowed her to treat large animals on-site. With her long blond hair, athletic style and fresh-faced beauty, Mackenzie was as authentic a person as she'd ever met.

Could she say the same for herself? Probably not. She wasn't sure who she was anymore. Hadn't known for years. And lately, she wanted to find out exactly what Ashlinn Burnier was all about.

"When is the movie thing?" Ashlinn acted like she was actually considering it. She wasn't.

"This Saturday." Mackenzie clasped her hands and stretched them over her head. "Ugh. My shoulders have been so tight lately. Anyway, Cade and I are getting there early to help Erica and Dalton set up the screen and make sure the food vendors park in the right area. I hope Lindsey doesn't spring any wild animals on us this go-round. It was pandemonium when the critters got loose last year."

Ashlinn chuckled softly. She'd heard all about the raccoon incident from the previous summer.

"It's at Memorial Park, right?" Before Mackenzie had arrived, Ashlinn had finished entering information into the spreadsheet. No more work was getting done today, so she saved it and closed the program. She'd made it through two hours of work without a single alert from Peanut. Felt like a victory.

"Yes. Cade and I will gladly pick you up. Everyone sits on the lawn. Brooke and Dean are leaving the twins with her mom—the girls' father was killed in a training mission shortly after they were born. When Dean moved back to town last November, Brooke reconnected with him. Their wedding should be a good time. Have you met her brother, Marc Young?"

"Not yet."

"Their mom owns Annie's Bakery. Marc's wife, Reagan, isn't sure about bringing the baby, so I don't know if they'll be there. Do you know Trent Lloyd and Gracie French?"

"Gracie stopped by the center with the girls."

"Aren't they adorable? Gracie was worried Noelle would get scared from the special effects, but the older two girls insisted they were all attending. Everyone loves this event. The entire town shows up for it."

Ashlinn swallowed the fear and insecurity lodged in her throat. That was what she was afraid of. The entire town would witness her flat on her back, passed out for who knew how long. No thanks.

"I don't know. Last week was pretty rough. I don't want to overdo it."

Patrick appeared in the doorway. "I didn't hear you come in, Mackenzie. Would you check Candy for me? She's favoring her left paw. I didn't feel anything out of the ordinary in her right foreleg. Maybe you'll know what's wrong."

"Sure." Mackenzie stood and turned back to Ashlinn. "Text or call me if you change your mind. I'll come get you and Peanut right before the movie starts."

"Are you going to the Shakespeare thing, Ashlinn?" Patrick's eyebrows arched.

"Um, probably not. I'm trying to take it easy." She gathered her tote and tumbler of water. "I'm taking off. I'll let you know tomorrow if I'm coming in or not."

"Thanks. If you do, I'll have Bandit continue working with you like he did earlier. I feel good about his progress."

"Me, too." She went over to Peanut, helping him into the harness. Then she grabbed the handle. "You ready, boy?"

Out in the sunshine, she adjusted her grip on his harness before telling him they were going on patrol. The command let him know he was supposed to heel unless her blood pressure plunged. If that happened, he'd block her path until she sat on the ground. They crossed the parking lot.

The Shakespeare movie would have appealed to her in college before her health had collapsed. She'd loved going to community events—summer concerts in the park, farmers markets, festivals. Last fall, she'd mentioned to her mom she'd like to go to an apple fest in a nearby town. The woman had acted like she'd requested to skydive without a parachute. And, truthfully, Ashlinn had been somewhat relieved to stay home. Who knew what might happen if she tried to navigate crowds?

At the stop sign, she checked for traffic, and she and Peanut crossed the road. Her mom and dad still called a few times each day, but lately, they hadn't sounded as panicky. Yes, her mother had overreacted to her visiting Ty's ranch, and the following day Ashlinn had had to listen to a ten-minute lecture on knowing her limits. Then, her mom had gone off on a new tangent, worrying about what Ashlinn would do come winter.

Ashlinn and Patrick had already discussed it. He would pick up her and Peanut and take them home on the days she came in. When she'd told her mother winter wouldn't be a big deal, she'd been met with a long, cold silence.

Dad hadn't been much better. He'd thrown out what-if scenarios and none of them had been good. What if Patrick got sick or was out of town? What if her house lost power? What if Peanut slipped on ice and took her down with him?

Just thinking about it made her grimace. As soon as she got inside her house, she removed Peanut's harness. The weather was perfect to sit out back in one of the chairs Ty had brought over.

This time she'd be smarter about it. She strapped on the monitor, grabbed a half-eaten bag of chips and her tumbler of water. Swiped the novel Christy had given her and called for Peanut.

As soon as she'd stretched out on the lounger, she closed her eyes, savoring the warm sun on her skin. Minutes ticked by as she relaxed. This was living.

"Knock, knock." Ty's low voice made her eyelids fly open. What was he doing here? And why was her heartbeat going thump, thump?

"Come in." She waved him to open the fence gate. He entered the yard, closing the gate behind him and took a seat on the lounger next to her. He had a package in his hand.

"I've never seen you in shorts." She grinned, pointing to his attire.

"I don't wear them often." He gave her a self-deprecating smile as he extended his legs on the lounger. The T-shirt, athletic shorts and running shoes looked good on him, as did the baseball hat. "Feels weird without my cowboy boots and hat."

"I'm sure." She nodded to the box he'd set on the side table. "What's that?"

"The flyers. Thought you'd like to see them." He passed it to her. She adjusted the back of the lounger upright and lifted the lid, taking the top flyer out.

The colors and layout looked amazing. "It's perfect. Exactly what we ordered."

"Yeah. I'm happy with how they turned out."

"Now what?" She placed the box on the grass between the chairs.

"Mom's been all over town this week asking for donations for the silent auction. She volunteered to drop these off to all the local businesses, too."

"That's really nice of her." Peanut came over but not to alert her. She wrapped her arm around him and kissed the top of his head. "You're a good boy."

Ty tilted his head slightly. "You been okay this week?"

"Yep. Back to normal." She nodded. "Well, my normal."

"That's good."

"I suppose you're going to the Shakespeare movie." She took a drink of water. "Mackenzie asked me to join them."

"Are you going?" He frowned. At the thought of her at the film? Or that she might be attending with Cade and Mackenzie?

"No. I don't think so."

"I'm not going, either."

"Why not?"

He shrugged. "Not my thing."

"Liar," she teased. "You told me you liked the special effects in the movie trailer."

"You remembered that?"

"Of course." Did the man have any clue that she'd hung on his every word since meeting him? "You should go."

"If I go, you should go, too."

"I couldn't."

"Same here."

"Ty…" She dragged out his name.

"Ashlinn…" He matched her tone. She laughed. "I'll go if you go."

"That's not fair," she said.

"Why not?"

"You don't have to worry about strangers seeing you pass out."

"You don't have to worry about everyone in town coming up to you and acting like you've been living in a cave for six years."

"Is that what's holding you back?"

"I don't know." He plucked a blade of grass from the ground and twirled it between his fingers. "I guess I don't get out all that much."

"Why not?" She shouldn't be surprised, but she was. Yet here he was. Hanging out with her. She was flattered.

"I like to cook at home or grab takeout. I'm not a recluse or anything. I go to church. Groceries. The feedstore. I hang out at Cade's sometimes, and I visit my grandma at the nursing home once a week."

She studied his handsome face, those solemn eyes. It seemed a shame he wasn't enjoying life to the fullest. Ty was missing out on all his hometown had to offer. From their previous conversations, she was certain he'd get a kick out of the local festivals and events. Maybe he needed a good excuse to get out more. Could she be that excuse? But if she was, could she handle being out and about?

"I tell you what, Ty Moulten. I think you and I *should* go to the movie this weekend."

"What?" He clearly hadn't been expecting her to suggest it. "No. It's too much for you."

She'd ignore that comment. Reminded her a little too much of her parents. "We'll spread out a quilt, bring the dogs. It'll be fun." Fun? More like stressful. And exhausting. Her stomach churned. While she would like to look forward to it, her anxiety wouldn't let her.

"But what if you faint? What if you get sick?"

"I'll lie on the quilt like I do at home." Maybe it wouldn't be as bad as she thought. The movie wouldn't start until it was getting dark out. And they'd be on the lawn. She could simply rest on a blanket if Peanut alerted her. Her nerves started to settle. "I don't think anyone would even notice me fainting if what Mackenzie said is true."

"About what?"

"Everyone sits on the lawn facing the screen. No one will be paying me any attention." She hoped they wouldn't be, anyway.

Was she being naive thinking she could handle a movie in the park?

"Okay. You talked me into it. We'll go. I'll get everything set up beforehand, then I'll pick up you and Peanut. But you need to prepare yourself for one thing."

"What?"

"Everyone *will* pay attention to us. It's a small town. They'll notice."

"Oh." She wasn't sure she liked the sound of that. "So if I pass out, people will talk?"

He nodded.

"Maybe it's for the best. Get it out of the way. I'm sure most of them know about my condition at this point."

"Are you sure you want to chance it?" he asked.

No. But she'd do it for him. "Yeah. I'm sure."

"Could anything trigger you to get worse?" He tossed the blade of grass behind him.

"Permanently?"

"Yeah."

"I'm not sure. Right now I'm managing the fainting and stomach problems."

"What made you bedridden back when you lived with your folks?"

"I wasn't able to keep food down, and without Peanut, I had no warning when I fainted. Every time I tried to stand I would pass out. Eating was impossible—I missed most meals. I was so weak I couldn't do much of anything. I lived on meal replacement drinks, and I relied on my parents for everything. The health I'm enjoying now? I'm not guaranteed it will last."

He nodded as if he understood. "I want to make sure I'm prepared. Is there anything else I should be concerned about?"

"Like what?" She'd told him her symptoms. What more did he need to know?

"Your blood pressure—could you have a heart attack? What about seizures?"

"My heart's fine. I've never had a seizure."

His expression cleared in relief. She hadn't realized he worried about all that. Had he built up her disease to be more dangerous than it was?

"Right now, passing out and injuring myself in the process are my only real threats. Everything else I can manage."

"What if it gets worse again? What if you can't get out of bed or keep food down?"

"Don't say that." She winced in a playful manner, trying to lighten the mood. "I don't know what will happen.

I could get worse, and I suppose I'd have to move back in with my parents."

"I don't want you to."

"I don't want to, either."

What had started out as a light conversation had shifted to something deeper. She realized he cared about her—and not as a friend—as something more.

Ty knelt next to her. Then he tenderly ran the edge of his finger down the hair framing her face. She could only stare wide-eyed at him, sensations firing her nerve endings.

"You're so beautiful, Ashlinn. I want to kiss you."

He thought she was beautiful? Wanted to kiss her? She couldn't think of a single reason to object. "Then kiss me."

His hand slipped behind her neck, and he cradled the back of her head as he brought his mouth to hers. She tentatively touched his cheek, smooth from shaving, warm from the heat of the day, and gasped at the feel of his lips on hers. He smelled like leather and bodywash. Tasted like mint. She kissed him back, feeling more alive than she had in years. Maybe ever.

Then he drew back. His dark eyes brooded as they glimmered with unspoken words—he liked her. A lot.

The feeling was mutual.

He rose and backed up a step. Regrets crashed over her. She shouldn't be flirting with Ty. Shouldn't be kissing him or leading him on.

He didn't see marriage in his future, and neither did she, in hers.

But if their circumstances were different...

She knew better than to saddle this cowboy with her health problems. He'd been devastated when he lost Zoey. He deserved someone who didn't need constant care—a woman who could sit next to him at church and go to a local festival and be a true partner to him. She'd never be that woman.

He never should have kissed her.

Saturday evening, Ty adjusted the quilt on the lawn of Memorial Park. He'd brought a cooler full of ice and beverages, two camping chairs and a bag with an assortment of snacks. All he had to do was drive to her place and bring her here. And he would. Soon.

But he wasn't ready just yet.

He'd spent all day yesterday and today thinking about how soft her lips had been against his. How sweet she'd tasted. How her fingers had touched his cheek so tenderly. How she made him feel like a strong man instead of a weak hermit.

But he wasn't strong. He was scared. Too caught up in his own problems to leave his house and socialize. Too insecure to face the town's questions and pity. Even now, he worried more about how people would react to seeing him than if Ashlinn would be safe.

He gave their spot a final once-over. Cade strode his way. "Good, you're set up next to us."

Like he'd had a choice in the matter.

"Mom's going to be up there with Charlene, Mary and some other ladies." Cade pointed ahead to where an entire row of camping chairs had been set up. "And I told Trent to sit on the other side of us."

Ty tried not to wince. Trent's three nieces were cute and all, but Ty hadn't been around kids much. Would they be running around, bothering Ashlinn?

"What about the twins?" he asked, bracing himself for Brooke and Dean and her two-year-old identical twin girls.

"Anne's babysitting them. Reagan and Marc might bring baby Elizabeth."

"Don't tell me. Next to us." He gulped.

Cade let out a guffaw. "No, dummy. They're up there next to Erica, Dalton and the boys."

"Then who's sitting here?" he asked.

"How should I know? Snoop around. Maybe there's a name." Cade nodded to the neat stack of supplies—a camping chair, cooler, rolled-up blanket. "I hope the weather holds."

"Me, too." Ty's phone alarm went off. "I've got to pick up Ashlinn."

"You bringing Fritz?"

"Yeah. He's with her now."

"All right, man. See you in a little while."

Ty kept his chin down as he strode to his truck. The park was filling up, and he didn't want to be stopped by anyone who had a bunch of questions.

As soon as he drove away, regrets filled him. Maybe he wasn't cut out for this. Too many things could go wrong. He was bound to get questions like, "Haven't seen you in years, where have you been?" and sympathetic smiles practically shouting, "He's finally getting over Zoey."

He wasn't getting over Zoey.

He'd never get over Zoey.

His hands strangled the steering wheel. He forced himself to loosen his grip. *Think about Ashlinn. She deserves a good time tonight.*

He half hoped she'd call the whole thing off. They could stay at her place, share a pizza, enjoy a summer night under the lights he'd strung in her backyard—just them and the dogs. No people. No questions. No worries.

As soon as Ashlinn opened the door, all his objections galloped away. She had on a pink sundress, and her hair was pulled back into a half ponytail with the rest of her hair flowing down her back. To say she glowed would be an understatement. He forced himself to breathe. Man, she was stunning.

"You look pretty." He kept his hands by his sides. All he wanted to do was touch her.

Her cheeks flushed. "Thank you."

The urge to take her into his arms and kiss her again was overwhelming. Instead, he followed her inside and glanced around for the dogs. Both zoomed to him with their tails wagging. "Hey, guys. Ready to go to the park?"

"I know I am." She began getting Peanut's harness on him. "Unlike these two, I'm a little nervous."

"Yeah, me, too." His fingertips tapped like drumsticks against his thighs. Although the weather was warm, he'd opted for jeans and cowboy boots. Had to be as comfortable as possible. He found Fritz's leash and attached it.

"I think I'm all set."

"What else do you need? Do you have your blood pressure cuff?"

She patted the tote bag she'd slung over her shoulder. "Right here."

He hesitated as he stared into her eyes. "We don't have to do this, you know. Say the word. We can stay home."

"Part of me wants to stay here." She blinked up at him.

"All right, then, no problem. We stay." It was what he wanted, so why did he feel let down?

"I don't think so." A smiled flirted in the corners of her mouth. "A bigger part of me wants to go."

He couldn't argue with that. "Okay. Then it's a yes. Let's go."

Five minutes later, he'd parked on a side street and held Fritz's leash in one hand and Ashlinn's tote in the other. She stayed close to him, keeping a firm grip on the handle of Peanut's harness.

"I've never been to the park before."

"It's a nice park. The legacy club enlists volunteers to plant flowers each summer, and one of the high school teachers started a program for students to keep the gazebo and sign painted."

"Everyone works together to make Jewel River nice. That's pretty amazing."

"It wasn't always this way. To be honest, the town had gotten run-down over the years. When Erica Cambridge moved to town, she started the Jewel River Legacy Club. The members identified the areas where the town could use improvement, and that's how Patrick and Mackenzie ended up here. My brother was in charge of calling several veterinarians, and he talked Mackenzie into moving."

"And now they're married."

"Yeah, it worked out great."

"It sure did."

They turned the corner and joined the crowd finding spots on the lawn. Dusk was falling. Ty pointed ahead. "We're over there. How are you feeling? Need to rest or anything?"

"I don't think so. Peanut would let me know if I did."

A couple spotted him and waved. "Well, look who's here! Ty Moulten. It's been forever since we've seen you."

He inwardly groaned. He'd graduated from high school with Katie Smith. He believed her husband's name was Bryce. He gave them both a nod. "Good to see you."

If he thought that would suffice, he was mistaken.

Katie, a short, full-figured brunette, blocked their path. "Who's your friend?"

Why couldn't she let them go in peace? He forced himself to be polite. "Katie, this is Ashlinn. Ashlinn, Katie. And Bryce, right?"

The guy nodded. Weighed down with camping chairs, a

cooler and a few large bags, Bryce didn't attempt to shake hands. Oblivious to her husband's burden, Katie took in the situation. "Oh, you have a service dog."

"I do." Ashlinn's serene tone lowered Ty's stress a tad.

"What's it for?"

Ty wanted to snap that it was none of her business, but Ashlinn merely gave Peanut a loving glance. "I have a disease that makes me faint a lot. Peanut keeps me safe."

"Peanut? What a cute name. He's adorable." Katie turned to Bryce. "Look at his face. We need to get a golden retriever."

"We need to find a place to sit," Bryce said dryly. "The movie's going to be starting soon."

"Fine." She addressed Ty and Ashlinn. "It was good to see you."

Ty grunted, not caring if she thought he was rude. They slowly picked their way around people to get to their spot. After setting the tote next to one of the camping chairs, Ty offered Ashlinn his arm to help steady her as she sat. She smiled up at him in gratitude, and his heartbeat pounded. When she looked at him like that, he'd probably do anything for her.

"You made it!" Mackenzie got up to hug Ashlinn. Cade scooped up Fritz and lavished the dog with attention. Then Mackenzie turned to Ty. "Cade told me you were coming, and I said I'd believe it when I saw it."

"Ty!" His mom spotted him. She and her posse of middle-aged and retired women got out of their seats to bustle over to them. Soon, he and Ashlinn were surrounded. A cold sweat broke out on his forehead.

There was no way out. He had a recurring nightmare where a serial killer strangled him and tossed his body in a creek to drown. This was worse.

"Your mother told me you were coming, and I didn't believe her." Mary Corning shook her head in wonder. "Look at you, Ty Moulten. At the Shakespeare movie. I never thought I'd see the day."

He didn't know what to say. He stood there like a trapped animal.

With both hands reaching out, Mary motioned for him to give her a hug. "Get over here."

He made the mistake of glancing at his brother as he stepped into her embrace. Cade's shoulders were shaking in silent laughter. Ty shot him a lethal glare, then gave into Mary's aggressive hug.

One of the other women shouted, "Dorothy, look! Ty left his ranch."

Charlene came over, making a fuss, and his mother took the opportunity to trap Ashlinn in conversation.

That did it. He was sweeping Ashlinn in his arms, calling the dogs, marching to the truck and driving straight back to her house.

"Ty!" Dorothy wrapped him into a bear hug before he could escape. She placed her palms against both his cheeks like he was two years old. "Your mother said you were getting out more, but I thought it was wishful thinking. I knew time would heal your wounds. I told her, 'You wait, he'll get back to himself, it just takes time,' more than once, didn't I, Christy?"

"Leave the man alone. He's not a stuffed toy." Clem appeared to his left. "He's got better things to do than get fussed over by you biddies."

Saved by… Clem? Ty flashed him a stare full of thanks. Clem gave him a firm nod.

"I haven't seen him anywhere other than church in years." Mary popped a fist on her hip. "I've got a lot of hugs to catch up on. Ty, honey, you've always been one of my favorite cowboys."

Would it be blasphemous to pray that God would make him disappear? That he could vanish into thin air?

"Hey, Ty?" Cade's voice came from behind him.

Ty turned. "What?"

Mackenzie was helping Ashlinn sit down on the quilt as Peanut licked Ashlinn's hand. Ignoring his mother's friends, he crossed over and got down on one knee. Was she okay? Everyone was too close.

"Give us some space, will you?" he said gruffly.

"Come on, let's get back to our seats," his mother said, extending her arms to herd everyone away. "The movie is about to start."

"Cover." Ashlinn patted her lap for Peanut to sit on her legs. The dog did and panted up at her. She stroked his fur. "Good boy."

"You okay, Ash?" Ty fumbled opening the tote and rooted around for her blood pressure monitor. Once he found it, he attached it to her wrist. Then he reached across her for her tumbler of water and handed it to her. She stared at him through grateful eyes and took a long drink.

"What do you need me to do?" Cade asked.

Ty glanced up at him. "Keep Fritz for me for now, would you?"

He nodded, taking the leash. Cade and Mackenzie went to their camping chairs next to them, and Cade lifted Fritz onto his lap. Ty shifted to sit next to Ashlinn, slipping his hand around her lower back to keep her steady.

"Whatever you need, I'm here," he whispered. A hint of flowers and vanilla teased his senses.

"Thanks, Ty." She leaned her head against his shoulder.

He clenched his jaw, honored at her trust, wishing he could cure her.

He'd do anything to keep this woman safe. Even if it meant enduring another hugging session from his mom's friends. He'd still prefer to be strangled by a serial killer and tossed in a creek, though.

"Welcome, everyone!" Near the huge projector screen set up on the lawn, Erica Cambridge held a microphone. "Thank you all for coming. Tonight is our third annual Shakespeare-in-the-Park film, and we have Joey Zane and Lindsey Parker to thank for it. So find yourself a seat and get ready for *Taming of the Shrew: Throw Her into Jewel River.*"

"Still doing okay?" Ty asked Ashlinn. Peanut had gotten off her lap and was sitting next to her.

"Much better."

"Want to stay on the quilt or move to the chair?" He tenderly brushed a lock of hair behind her ear.

"I want to stay right here." She glanced at him, and her shining eyes stole his breath.

"Here, you can lean against me." He moved to sit behind her so she could lean back against his chest. He wrapped his arms around her, struck by how right it felt to have her in his arms. The ends of her hair lifted in the breeze, and Peanut lowered himself to rest his chin on his paws.

As the sun disappeared on the horizon, the movie began.

An overhead view of the prairie and the river appeared on the screen. A low male voice began narrating. "Beautiful, gentle Bianca can't get married until her sharp-tongued sister, Katherina, lands herself a husband. Their daddy, Baptista Minola, turns away the cowboys who pine for Bianca. Local rancher, Hortensio, convinces his friend Petruchio to overlook Katherina's mean ways. If he does, he'll get a wad of cash to marry her. And so our story begins..."

Lars Denton, in old-timey clothes and a cowboy hat, entered a log cabin where Henry Zane, Joey's grandfather, was sitting at a table.

"Ahh, rancher Baptista, rumor has it your daughter Katherina is quite a catch." Lars—Petruchio—took off his hat and sat across from him.

"Katherina?" He spat on the floor. "She ain't for you, boy."

Ashlinn turned back to look at him with a confused expression. "This is more of a loose adaptation, huh?"

"Very loose."

Ty kept his arms around her as the movie progressed. Ashlinn startled when a tornado chased Petruchio and Katherina riding horseback across the prairie, and she tensed when Katherina argued with Petruchio, causing him to toss her over his shoulder and march to Jewel River. But he didn't throw her in.

The movie was choppy and strange, and Ty enjoyed every minute of it.

Finally, after a well-placed martial-arts kick to his shins, Petruchio pulled Katherina into his arms.

"Kiss me, Kate."

"Here?" Katherina asked. "In the middle of this dusty street? After I just kicked you?"

"Yes." Fireworks exploded over the couple as they kissed, and the words *The End* covered the screen.

Everyone on the lawn burst into applause and whistles. As they gathered their things, Ty realized Ashlinn hadn't fainted, and he'd survived the fussing by his mother's friends.

It had been the best night he'd had in a long time. All because of Ashlinn.

Chapter Eight

"Surprise!"

What were her mom and dad doing on her front porch? It had been exactly one week since the movie in the park, and Ashlinn couldn't stop thinking about Ty. And now her parents were here? She opened the door wider to give them both a hug. "You drove all the way from South Dakota?"

"We missed you, sweetheart." Carrying two large bags, her mother swept inside. Peanut wagged his tail for her to pet him. "Oh, and darling Peanut. Look at you." She set the bags down to scratch behind his ears.

"I'll bring everything in. Be right back." Dad winked and pivoted to go back down the porch steps. Ashlinn joined her mother in the living room.

Her parents had shown up on a Saturday afternoon. With no warning.

She should be happy. But…they'd assumed she didn't have plans. Not that she blamed them—what plans could she possibly have? She had no car. Of course she'd be home. But why not give her a heads-up? Then she could have cleaned— which was probably why they hadn't called. Mom wouldn't have wanted her to clean. Too worried it would take the wind out of her sails.

"The spare room is exactly the way you left it if you want

to put your things in there." Ashlinn tried to keep her tone cheery, but it upset her that they hadn't called in advance.

Her mother gave Peanut a final pat, then made her way to the kitchen and began removing items from one of the bags. "I picked up some of those crackers you liked so much when you were living with us."

"I didn't like them." The words came out clipped, and she couldn't seem to mask her irritation. "They were the only thing I could keep down."

"Oh, well, I figured you'd want them on hand. Especially after your recent stomach problems. Dad's bringing in a case of the nutrition drinks, too. Can't be too careful."

A wave of sadness crushed her. She took a seat at the table, not wanting to get emotional and hurt her mom's feelings. But really—what was she thinking? Bringing in supplies that only reminded her of a time she'd rather forget?

"What's wrong?" Her mom came over and placed the back of her hand against Ashlinn's forehead. She swatted the hand away. Her mother let out a huff. "What was that for?"

"I don't have a fever. I'm not sick. I don't need—" she waved to the bags "—crackers and gross nutrition drinks. I'm doing fine."

"For now." Her mother pulled out the chair kitty-corner to her and gave her a pointed stare. "You need to be prepared for when you're not well."

"Wow. You haven't seen me in a month, and the first thing you do is assume I'm getting worse. I'm not, Mom. If anything, I'm getting better."

The last part was a lie. She couldn't in good faith claim she was getting better. More like staying the same. She still passed out two to three times a day. On Tuesday, she'd been nauseous and had survived on broth and tea. But by Wednesday, she'd bounced back. And she'd gone into the training center twice this week. That had to count for something.

The front door opened with a creak, and the stomp of her dad's heavy footsteps faded down the hall to the spare room.

"I know you *want* to be better." Condescension dripped from her mother's tone. "It's natural to feel that way."

"Why are you talking to me like I'm twelve?"

Her mom straightened as she pursed her lips. "I'm not. Honestly, Ashlinn, I'm starting to wonder if you're even happy we came."

Guilt slid down her spine. "Of course I'm happy. You simply caught me off guard."

"Don't tell me you had big plans." Her mother shook her head, seeming to laugh at her own joke. That one hurt.

"Last weekend I did."

"What do you mean?"

"Jewel River hosted a movie in the park, and I went." She hadn't told her parents about it, knowing if she did, she'd get lectured.

The rapid blinking had Ashlinn girding herself for the speech sure to be on its way. "How on earth did you get there?"

"There. Everything's inside." Her father entered the room and took a seat across the table from her mom. His smile faded as he picked up on the tension. "What's wrong, Paula?"

At her mother's pinched face, Ashlinn spoke up. "I was just telling Mom about the movie in the park I went to last weekend."

"Oh yeah?" His forearms rested on the table. "What was the movie? Anything we've seen?"

"Oh no. Definitely not." Her spirits lifted at the memory. "A couple of local teens filmed it. They adapted a Shakespeare play."

"Which one?"

"*Taming of the Shrew.* Except they added a subtitle: *Throw Her into Jewel River.*"

Her dad's baffled expression lowered her tension.

"How did you get to the park?" Mom's tongue unraveled, and each word could have been chipped from ice.

"Ty brought me."

"The cowboy you've been hanging around?" Why did it sound like she was accusing Ashlinn of something?

"Yes. I'm helping him plan the fundraiser I told you about. It's in honor of his fiancée. She died a long time ago."

"Sounds like he's still in love with her if he's planning a dinner in her honor." She folded her hands primly. She'd said the same words more than once on the phone.

"He probably is." Ashlinn hated admitting it. Wanted to tell her mom that Ty had kissed her. But a kiss was just a kiss. It wasn't love. Wasn't an engagement ring. Wasn't forever. He didn't want forever. And she didn't think she could have it, anyway.

"And he's the one who took you to his ranch?"

"Yes."

An odd, strangled sound erupted from her mother's throat. And her father rapped his knuckles on the table. "When can we meet him?"

"They aren't dating, Dave." The woman got those words out rapid-fire.

"I didn't say they were." He gave her mom an annoyed glance. "I'd like to thank him for helping keep an eye on Ashlinn."

Did they think she was completely incapable of surviving on her own? Well...they might have a point.

Mom widened her eyes sarcastically. "Don't say that, Dave, or she'll accuse you of asking him to babysit her."

"Am I missing something?" her father asked.

Ashlinn inhaled and counted to three. Would have counted to five, but Peanut started licking her hand.

"Great. Now you're upset. This is what I was afraid of." Her mother stood and held out her hand. "I'll help you get to your fainting station."

"I can do it myself," she said quietly.

"Oh, yes, Miss Do-it-Herself." Her mother crossed her arms over her chest.

Ashlinn ignored her and brought the tumbler of water to the living room. Once she was on the floor, she dragged her weighted blanket over her lower legs.

Her parents joined her and sat on the couch. Peanut plopped down beside her.

"Maybe we should have a word with Patrick." Her mother tapped her chin. "Let him know you need to come in less often."

"You will do no such thing," Ashlinn said. Her mother had been here for all of ten minutes and had already pushed every one of her buttons. "I know my limits."

"But you don't need to work." Now her mother had shifted to concerned mode. The one that made Ashlinn want to grind her teeth and leave the room.

She petted Peanut and took another drink of water. "I like working. Bandit, a German shepherd Patrick's training, has been showing a lot of promise sensing my blood pressure spikes and dips. When I'm there, it helps him get better at recognizing the signs."

"Save your strength, honey. You can tell us about it later."

"I'm fine now. I'm on the floor. I think I know when I can talk." Maybe they needed a change in subject. "How is the dental office, Mom?" *Please take the hint and stop talking about my limitations.*

"Dr. Garrah broke his collarbone last month, and we've had to find another dentist to fill in until he's healed. It's caused a lot of headaches with scheduling…"

As her mother shifted to talk about her challenges as a dental hygienist, Ashlinn tuned out to focus on trying to prevent a faint. Peanut wandered over to his doggy bed, and Ashlinn realized her mom had stopped speaking.

"I would have expected you to faint by now." She looked puzzled.

"Sometimes my blood pressure goes back to normal without me passing out."

"You don't faint?" Her mom sounded baffled.

"Not every time. Most of the time, I do." Maybe she shouldn't have admitted the last part. Confusion was clouding her judgment. She loved her parents. She should be happy they were here. But so far, her nerves had been grated raw.

"Why don't I order some food for us?" Dad pulled out his phone and began swiping. "What sounds good?"

"How long are you staying?" Ashlinn hadn't meant for it to come out so quickly.

"Just tonight." Her mother's face seemed to age ten years. "We'll be on our way home tomorrow. We both have to work on Monday."

Twenty-four hours. She could do a day. "How about pizza?"

"I'll order two." Dad glanced at her. "You can call Ty and ask him to come over and join us. I'd like to meet him."

"Really?" She wasn't sure how she felt about it.

"Dave, don't put her on the spot. It's not like they're dating."

But they could be dating. Not now…but…someday. Yeah, right. She was stuck with AAG. This was her life.

"He's already lost one fiancée," her mom said. "Why would he want to get involved with someone who has ongoing health problems? I shudder to think about how tough life was for you only a few years ago, Ash. I don't want you getting hurt. Think about how hard it would be if you grew close to him only to have him leave you when your health gets worse."

"Who said my health was going to get worse?" And who said Ty would leave her if it did?

"Don't act like I'm the bad guy. We all know it could."

"Leave her be, Paula." Her dad shook his head in exasperation. "I'll call in the order. You call your cowboy."

Her cowboy. She wished.

No matter how much her mom's words hurt, Ashlinn recognized the truth in them. Ty *had* already lost a fiancée. Ashlinn's health *could* take a turn for the worse. And it *would* be devastating to get close to him only to have him walk away.

"Hand me my phone. I'll see if he's free."

Ty shouldn't have agreed to come over to meet her parents. Should have given her an excuse like he'd been doing with his mom and brother for years, not that they'd ever listened. But, no, he'd heard the strain in her voice when she'd invited him, and he'd known he couldn't decline. Not when she needed some moral support.

He parked on the street and cut the engine. All week his mom had been raving about how her friends had been glad to see him getting out again and how pleased they were he was getting back to life. Like he'd been in a coma for the past six years or something. To be fair, they had a point.

Ty got out of the truck and shut the door with a bit too much force. His mother meant well. She'd wanted to encourage him, to help him see that people cared about him. But she'd failed.

Her calls and texts only served to highlight the reason he'd stayed away from town. Now that he was getting out more, it was obvious his devotion to Zoey was fading. He shouldn't be spending time with Ashlinn when he'd told himself he'd never get close to a woman again.

He'd lost too much. And he didn't want to lose again.

Taking long strides, he headed up the porch steps and knocked on the door. Voices argued inside. He couldn't make out what they were saying. The door opened, and a middle-aged man with a receding hairline and slight paunch appeared.

"You must be Ty." The man grinned and held out his hand. "Dave Burnier."

"Glad to meet you, sir." He shook his hand and followed him into the living room.

"This is Paula, Ashlinn's mother." Dave motioned to a pretty woman he assumed was in her late fifties. She nodded. Ty detected skepticism in her stare. Or maybe it was suspicion. Hesitation? Whatever it was, she didn't seem to like him much.

"Thanks for coming." Ashlinn came over and gave him a quick hug. He fought the urge to hold her close and whisper it would all be okay.

"Thanks for inviting me."

"We ordered a couple of pizzas. Why don't you and I go pick them up?" Dave held up a key fob. "I'll drive."

"He doesn't have to go with you, Dad."

"No, it's fine," Ty said. "I'll go."

Her father grinned. "We'll be right back. Why don't you two pick out a movie or something?"

Ty suppressed a grimace. This wasn't how he'd planned on spending his Saturday night. All day he'd forced himself to not call Ashlinn. They'd already spent three evenings together this week to work on the fundraiser. The planning could have been wrapped up in one short session. He couldn't seem to stay away from her.

Ashlinn had picked out decorations and ordered inexpensive centerpieces for the tables. She'd also updated him on the guest list. They were expecting it to grow next Friday when they got a final head count. And he'd briefed her on all the donations his mom and Charlene had gotten from local businesses.

"So you've lived here your entire life, huh?" Dave asked as they climbed into his SUV. Green leaves rustled in the trees overhead. The hot weather spelled trouble. Ty wouldn't be surprised if a lightning storm brewed.

"Yes, I grew up on a ranch east of town."

"You still work there? Ashlinn mentioned visiting your ranch."

Ty explained how he came to own the ranch as her father drove to town.

"Sounds like you're a real cowboy."

"You could say that." Ty tried to stay relaxed. "I refuse to ride bulls, though. I'm not getting myself killed."

Dave chuckled.

"What do you do for a living?" Ty asked.

"I'm surrounded by numbers. I work for a financial company. Mostly detail work."

"Do you like it?" Ty couldn't imagine sitting in an office dealing with numbers all day. Every morning, he looked forward to taking a thermos of coffee out to the stables while the sun rose. After a briefing with his ranch hands, he'd saddle his horse or hop in the UTV, and they'd all set off to take care of the cattle.

"I can't complain." Her father shrugged as he pulled up to the pizza place. "Pays the bills."

Can't complain. Echoes of Ty's father saying those exact

words pierced him. He didn't think about his father very often anymore. He missed him, though.

What would his dad think of Ashlinn? He'd probably love her. Who wouldn't?

The pizzas were ready, and Ty offered to pay, but Dave insisted. Within a few minutes, they were back in the SUV.

"How is Ashlinn? Really?" He waited for a truck to pass before pulling out on the road.

"Good." Where was he going with this?

"The fainting spells. They're under control?" He glanced sideways at Ty.

"Um, yes? I guess." His shoulders tensed. He didn't know if they were or not. "I don't know what under control means."

Dave sighed. "I worry about her."

"I do, too." He hadn't meant to admit it out loud.

"I'm glad." He nodded, then shot a sheepish stare his way. "I mean, I'm glad she has people here to help."

"She does. Me. Patrick, Mackenzie, my mom, any of our friends. We look out for her."

They drove in silence for a while. Then Dave sighed. "It's only fair to warn you this is the best her life has been in years. We don't know if it will last."

The words hit his gut like a water balloon on concrete. "What do you think is going to happen?"

"I'm not sure. But I stood by helpless for years when she couldn't stand up without passing out. Couldn't eat without getting sick. Couldn't make it to another room without our help because she was so weak. I don't want her hurt if you're on the fence because of her disease. Her current health *is* the best-case scenario we prayed for. It's not perfect, and it might not last."

"I understand." He did. Her dad didn't want her stuck in

Jewel River with all her health problems *and* a broken heart. "We're friends. And friends look out for each other."

"Yes, they do. We're thankful she has friends." He parked in Ashlinn's driveway. "We also know that when things tip to more than friends, there's a greater chance of getting hurt."

Ty bristled, not enjoying the implications behind the warning.

"I've been honest with Ashlinn. We're friends. Just friends." If that didn't close the topic, he didn't know what would. But was it true? He'd been crossing the friendship line for a while now. And last he'd heard—friends didn't kiss each other.

"Good to know." Dave nodded. "Let's get in there and eat."

Ty grabbed the pizzas from the backseat. As he and Dave entered the living room, he gave Ashlinn a slight nod to ease the concern in her eyes. After they'd gotten settled around the table, they said grace.

Paula addressed Ty. "Your ranch—it's nearby?"

The slice of pizza in his hand hovered near his mouth. His gut clenched, and he put the pizza back on the plate without taking a bite. It appeared the interrogation wasn't over. In fact, it was probably just beginning.

"Depends on how you define nearby. It's about thirty minutes from town."

"Oh." The word managed to simultaneously convey disappointment and judgment. Ty had a new appreciation for his own mother. Sure, she meddled nonstop, but she would genuinely welcome anyone off the street if he told her they were friends—she wouldn't view them with suspicion. "Not many neighbors around, I gather?"

"No. Just me and my herd. My brother is a short drive away. I have a few ranch hands. They don't live on my property, though."

"I see."

"You should come out and see it sometime." Had he really said that? He didn't invite people over. And these people didn't seem to like him.

Ashlinn's face lit up. "It's beautiful. All that prairie. And you can see the mountains in the distance. It's so relaxing out there."

"I'm sure it is." Paula's smile didn't reach her eyes. "Awfully far away if something were to happen, though."

"Like what?" Ashlinn's voice had a jagged edge.

"You know." Her mother's eyes glinted as she stared at her. The tension in the air made his toes curl.

Dave cleared his throat. "Maybe next time we come, we can all take a drive out and see your ranch, Ty."

"I'd like that." He'd hate that. But what else could he say? These were Ashlinn's parents.

Their assumptions were backing him into a corner.

They didn't trust him.

"Ashlinn mentioned you live in a small town, too." Ty took a bite, determined to get out of the spotlight.

"Yes, not quite as small as Jewel River, but it suits us." Paula's face softened. "I've never been one for the city."

"Me neither," Ty said.

"I don't know if I'd like the city or not," Ashlinn said. "I've never spent much time in one."

"They're okay." Dave shrugged. "I travel for work sometimes, and I'm always glad to come home."

"I guess we all have that in common," Ty said. At least they had something in common.

When they finished eating, they sat in her living room and talked for a few hours. Then Ty excused himself, telling them he had to get back for Fritz. On the porch, Ashlinn gave him a quick hug.

"I'll see you in a day or two." More than ever, he wanted to hug her, to hold her, to kiss her again. The way her parents acted around him had brought up his defenses, though.

Ashlinn's eyes were shining as she nodded. Worry rippled through them. "Thanks for coming."

"Of course."

As he drove home, things he'd been pushing away reared up. His dad, for one. Pete Moulten had been gone for a decade. His father—his hero. And that brought to mind how close he'd been to Zoey's parents. They'd welcomed him into their family, too.

In the end, what had it mattered? He no longer had a relationship with them. They'd vanished from his life the same as Zoey had.

Would it be the same with Ashlinn? With her parents?

Her parents didn't like him. That much was obvious. If he lived closer to town, maybe they'd consider accepting him. But he wasn't living in town. Ever. His ranch was his life.

The hornet's nest of emotions from experiences he'd suppressed stung him. He needed some advice. Needed a way to make sense of everything.

Tomorrow, after church, he was going to pull the pastor aside and make an appointment to talk to him. Pastor Bracken had counseled him after Zoey died. Maybe he could help him now. Ty had a feeling he needed all the help he could get.

Chapter Nine

"Thanks for taking time out to talk." Ty sat in Pastor Bracken's office Sunday afternoon.

"Anytime, Ty." The white-haired man behind the desk had an easygoing manner. "What's on your mind?"

Where to start? He didn't know. "Everything's jumbled. I'm not sure where to begin."

"Is everything okay at the ranch?"

"Yes, the cattle are in their summer pasture. They should be able to graze all winter without me having to supplement their feed too much."

"The rain we had this spring helped."

"It sure did." His anxiety unraveled bit by bit. "I just finished cutting hay. Still fixing fences."

"Never-ending job." The pastor leaned back with a kind smile. "Work doesn't seem to be the issue."

"No, it's personal," Ty said. "I don't think about my father too much, but yesterday he came to mind. And when I thought about him, I couldn't help but think about Zoey's family. When I was part of it. It's like my dad and the Daniels family are intertwined."

The pastor nodded encouragingly.

"I get this kind of bubble in my throat. Hurts. I don't understand it."

"You were close to your dad. You were close to Zoey's family, too."

"I guess I miss them. It's strange, though. Why would I miss them now? I mean, I've been making an effort to spend more time in town. I'm around more people now than I have been in years. What gives?"

"Grief can be funny that way."

"But Zoey's parents are alive. I'm not grieving them."

"Do you ever talk to them anymore?"

Ty shook his head.

"Another loss." The grooves in the pastor's forehead deepened. "Why do you think they've been on your mind?"

"I don't know." Maybe he did. "The fundraiser?"

"You say that like it's a question."

"I've been spending time with Ashlinn Burnier. Her parents are in town. I wasn't expecting to meet them, and it didn't go all that well."

"Are you two getting close?"

"Not like that," he said hastily. "We're friends. She's helping me plan the fundraiser."

"Marjorie and I have tickets. Should be a fun evening. And for a good cause."

"I appreciate your support." Ty took a moment to process his thoughts. The beige walls of the office held framed photos of the pastor and his family. Three sons, two daughters, lots of grandkids. They all looked so happy up there. "After meeting her parents, I was driving home and got kind of upset thinking about my dad. Thinking about Zoey."

"You've lost people who were important to you. Your father. Your fiancée. Her parents. Getting close to new people puts us in a vulnerable position. You don't know—you might lose them the same as you lost the others."

Ty clenched his hands. Was that what was going on? Was he afraid to lose again?

"I think there's room for more people in your heart. I hope you'll pray about it. I'll pray for you, too."

"Would it be wrong to pray that God doesn't let more people into my heart?"

The pastor leaned forward, sympathy radiating from him. "God is love, Ty. As John 13:34 tells us, 'A new commandment I give unto you, that ye love one another; as I have loved you, that ye also love one another.'"

"But God's talking about general love. Loving your neighbor. Not *love* love."

"Are you talking about *love* love?" He tilted his head, and Ty squirmed at the scrutiny.

"No. I'm not." He almost convinced himself. Almost.

"Well, there you go." He opened his hands. "Nothing to worry about."

"Thanks, Pastor." He rose. The pastor stood as well and walked him to the door.

"Come back anytime. I'm here for you, Ty."

"Thank you."

They shook hands, and Ty strode down the hall and out to the parking lot. While the truck idled, he pondered over the conversation. The pastor made sense. He was supposed to love people. And he *had* lost his dad and Zoey and, in some ways, her parents. Maybe his memories were warning him not to get hurt.

He drove away, and as he left town, one thing pressed against his heart. He wasn't as against romantic love as he'd been before Ashlinn arrived. But he should be. He couldn't go getting attached to her. He wouldn't add another set of people who'd no longer be in his life a few years down the road.

The pastor wanted him to pray about adding more people

into his heart. It had taken him years to tiptoe into a some-what normal life. Adding more people to his life was scary. What if he lost them and ended up retreating to his ranch again? All the progress of the past weeks would be lost.

God, I need Your help moving forward. I don't want to get hurt again.

The green prairie grass waved in the breeze as he drove. He'd keep praying. And hope his attraction to Ashlinn would end quickly. He couldn't afford another loss.

All he wanted to do was get home to Fritz.

"Not going to lie, Patrick, that was a rough visit." Tuesday morning, Ashlinn sat on the floor of the training arena while Patrick worked with Bandit. Peanut was gnawing on a dental chew in the corner.

"They didn't call ahead, huh?"

"No, and Mom treated me like I was a toddler made of porcelain." She hugged her knees to her chest.

"What about your dad?"

"He seemed fine." Had he been, though? He'd acted kind of weird Saturday when Ty had been there. Her father wasn't one to grill strangers with personal questions, and he'd come awfully close to interrogating Ty.

"Did the stress wear you out?"

"What do you mean?"

"Did it make your symptoms worse?"

"No, I felt the same. I mean, I definitely had to bite my tongue more than once, and I forced myself to take deep breaths when I got annoyed." She'd gotten annoyed several times. That alone bothered her. "I feel bad. Mom and Dad did everything for me—they sacrificed so much for so long. I hate to come off as ungrateful."

"You're not. You're moving on. They will, too." His kind tone eased her guilt.

"They *are* moving on. I mean, their lives are back to normal. Now that they don't have to help me, they can do the things they used to. Focus on their jobs, go to the farmers market on Saturday mornings, plan trips."

"They can. But sometimes it's easier said than done. It's hard to trust it."

"Trust what?" She rested her chin on her knees.

"That it won't happen again. And I'm sure they're worried that if it does they won't be around to help you. They're in another state."

"I know. But I can't help it. What do they want me to do? Move back in with them on the off chance my health deteriorates? No thanks."

"No parent wants that." He winced. "If you moved back, you'd resent them."

"Resentment is the right word." She pondered her mother's attitude and all the things she'd said. "I think my mom resents me for not falling apart. It's like she expected my health to collapse and is disappointed I'm fine."

She hadn't put her impressions into words, and now that she had, they unnerved her. Peanut ambled over, sat next to her and stared. Patrick commanded Bandit over, too. The German shepherd loped straight to him.

"Ashlinn, will you have Peanut check you? Then you can command Bandit to do the same."

She nodded, petting Peanut. She held out her arm. "Check." He sniffed her hand, licked it lightly and remained sitting. "Good boy."

Then she held her other arm out to Bandit. "Check."

The dog smelled from her wrist to her elbow. "Good boy.

Good job, Bandit." She stroked his back, and Patrick gave
him a treat and praised him.

"Let's see if Candy shows any interest. Do you mind sitting tight while I get her?"

"I'm not going anywhere. I don't have much choice with
Peanut staring me down." It was funny. The dog always knew
when her blood pressure was changing, but he detected the
signs long before she felt anything. She ruffled Peanut's fur.
"You take care of me, huh, bud?"

Maybe she was being too hard on her mom. Her parents had been as helpless as she'd been when it came to her
fainting, and it had been scary. Peanut had given them all
peace of mind.

Patrick returned with Candy. Ashlinn repeated the process. Peanut licked her hand and hunkered down next to her.
Candy didn't seem to know what to do when Ashlinn commanded her to check, but she sat on her haunches nearby.

"I don't think this is her specialty." Patrick watched the
dog with a thoughtful expression. "She's well behaved. Patient. She might be good with an autistic client."

"Not all dogs share the same talents." Ashlinn stroked
Peanut's back with her right hand and Candy's with her left.
"She's calm and comforting me right now."

"Want me to get your water?" Patrick asked.

"Yes, please." As he walked away, she lightly shook out
her arms and hands to keep her blood flowing. Patrick returned with her tumbler of water. "Could you bring the chair
over?"

He set a folding chair in front of her. She lay back and put
her legs on the seat. Peanut got up and went over to Patrick.
Candy, on the other hand, lowered her body to the ground
and stared at Ashlinn.

"You're obsessed with me like Peanut before I faint." She

petted the dog's head. "Maybe you know more than you're letting on."

"You're good at this." Patrick watched them.

"At being flat on my back, waiting to pass out?" she teased.

"No. You're good with the dogs. They trust you. You're patient with them."

"I don't think of myself as patient."

"You should. You're a patient person."

"Tell that to my mom." Again, the guilt crept in. She wished their visit had gone better.

"Maybe you can remind yourself of your patience next time she's here." Patrick turned away. "I'm bringing Bandit over again. It will be good for him to repeat the checks and see you through the entire process."

Patrick was right. She could do a better job of controlling her emotions around her mother. She just didn't know if she had it in her. Maybe she needed to practice like the dogs with their training here.

Bandit zoomed to Peanut's spot, and for some reason, it tickled her funny bone. Surrounded by dogs. She loved it.

"See? He's got it. You're making my job easy," Patrick said. "I'm grateful you're here. There's nothing like real-life experience to train these dogs."

"They're getting plenty of that."

"Oh, I forgot to tell you—I think I've found a van to buy. It's four years old, low mileage and has a rear entry with an automatic lift. It's got everything I'm looking for."

"That's great!" She wished she could sit up, but she knew better than to attempt it. "I hope you'll have enough for a down payment after the fundraiser. I can hardly believe it's only two weeks away."

"Yeah. I sure appreciate Ty doing this. I hope the van will still be for sale."

"Do you think it won't be?"

"If it isn't, God will have something else for me."

"You have a lot of faith."

"God's been faithful. I'm blessed."

God had been faithful to her, too. She was blessed. Yet the desire for more—for something better—kept creeping up on her. Not a better house. Not even a driver's license or a car.

She wanted a future that included a husband. A baby or two. A quiet cowboy to hang out with in her backyard on a sunny day.

Closing her eyes, she shook her head slightly.

God, You've been faithful to me. Forgive me for wanting more.

Ty helped Fritz into his therapy-dog vest as he waited for Cade in the nursing home's parking lot. They had a standing date every Friday afternoon to visit their grandmother. Her Alzheimer's had been worsening for a few years. Some days she recognized them, and others she didn't. Ty struggled with these visits, though not because of Nana. The smell of harsh chemical cleaners and the moans of the patients got to him. If it wasn't for Cade, Ty doubted he'd ever come here. He appreciated the chance to catch up with his brother, though.

Cade's truck pulled into the spot next to his.

"You're early." He pocketed his keys and, grinning, gave Ty a half hug with Fritz between them. "How's this little guy?"

"He's good. I will never understand how a dog can burrow under a blanket in the heat of summer. Refuses to settle unless there's a blanket over him."

Cade chuckled. "That's a wiener dog for you. Mackenzie says they're all like that. I see he's wearing his vest today."

"Yeah, I asked Charlene if I could bring him. Showed her

his Canine Good Citizen certificate. She agreed as long as he's wearing the vest." The dog's big brown eyes stared up at him, and the easy way his tongue panted told Ty the dog was perfectly content to be in his arms.

"It helps him know he's on duty," Cade said. "Does for Tulip, anyhow."

Neither of them made a move to head to the entrance. Puffy white clouds chugged across the blue sky. These were the days Ty longed for in January when ice storms blew in and the subzero temperature could shatter glass.

"How is the fundraiser shaping up? Need anything from me at this point?"

"Actually, yes, I could use something." He'd brought supper to Ashlinn yesterday, and he'd realized he still didn't have an emcee. "We don't have an emcee. You're good at public speaking."

Cade's chest puffed out. "Got that right."

"We both know I'm not." He didn't bother deflating his brother's ego, not when he needed a favor. "Would you do it?"

"What's involved?"

Fritz squirmed to be let down, and Ty lowered him to the asphalt. With the leash in hand, he began strolling toward the entrance of the one-story, brick building.

"Thank everyone for coming. Ask them to get seated. Announce updates on the silent auction. That sort of thing."

Cade opened one of the glass double doors, and Ty and Fritz entered the hallway. "I'll be the emcee on one condition."

Narrowing his eyes, Ty turned to him. Whatever Cade suggested, Ty could guarantee he wouldn't like it. "What is it?"

"You need to be the one to open the event. Welcome everyone. Tell them about Zoey. Talk about Howard Training Center. Introduce them to Ashlinn, so they can see how the dogs help real people. This is your baby—they'll appreciate hearing from you directly."

Cade spoke the truth. Still scared him to death, though.

"I'm no good at public speaking. I failed every oral book report I had to give in school."

Cade slung his arm over Ty's shoulders. "That was a million years ago. You're older now. You can handle it."

"I don't think I can." They approached the desk, where Charlene stood in her scrubs.

"You can. You will." Cade dropped his arm by his side. "Hello, Charlene. How is Nana today?"

"Well, look at you two. A sight for sore eyes, I tell you. If more single gals knew Jewel River had such handsome cowboys around, they'd move here in a heartbeat."

Ty was used to Charlene's flattery and ignored it.

"Too bad I'm taken." Cade pretended to dust his knuckles on his shoulder. "But Ty here could use a lady."

"I don't need a lady."

"Not anymore, you don't." Charlene beamed. "You and Ashlinn looked cozy together at the movie in the park."

That was not what he meant, but he didn't have the energy to argue.

"Here's our Fritzie!" Charlene clapped her hands as she came around the desk. She crouched in front of Fritz, who was sitting like the good dog he was. "How's our little man? You're looking handsome in your spiffy vest."

When she'd finished lavishing Fritz with attention, she straightened and hitched her chin toward the hall. "Miss Trudy's been pretty tired today."

Pretty tired meant lethargic and unlikely to recognize them. Ty had gotten used to it. Seemed Nana had more bad days than good lately.

"Thanks, Charlene." They headed to her room, pausing to

knock on the open door. Cade led the way inside, and Nana turned her head. Her bed was inclined so she could sit up.

"Hi, Nana." Cade hugged her first, then stepped away so Ty could give her a light embrace.

"I brought you a visitor." Ty scooped up the dog. "This is Fritz."

"My, my, he's a cute puppy." She smiled and held her arms out to take him.

"I'll set him on your lap."

"That's fine." She petted the dog as he stared up at her through understanding doggy eyes. "He's soft."

Ty and Cade sat in the chairs next to her bed.

"Where's Pete?" Nana continued to caress Fritz's back.

Ty glanced at Cade. His stomach always lurched when their grandmother acted like their dad was still alive. They'd talked to Charlene and the doctor about how to handle situations like this without upsetting her. Nana couldn't help the changes in her brain. It was best to go along with whatever she said and not argue with her. Would only agitate the woman.

"He's not around," Cade said.

"No?" Her forehead creased as she glanced their way. "Yesterday he told me he was going to the auction to buy some cattle. I thought he was supposed to be back today."

"Must have taken him longer than he expected." Cade made it look easy, handling her dementia. "What did you have for lunch?"

Confusion clouded her eyes. The paper-thin skin of her hand showed the veins as it stilled on Fritz's back. "I don't remember."

"Chicken?" Ty asked. Why would he assume she'd had chicken?

"Yes." Her face cleared as she nodded. "I should have saved a few bites for the doggy. He'd like it."

"He would," Ty said.

"Did Christy get Ty signed up for the mutton bustin' contest?"

Ty met Cade's confused gaze. His brother took pity on him. "Um, I'm not sure."

"Ask her next time you see her. Better yet, have her call me. I sewed him a special shirt to wear. That boy sure can ride a sheep for being so young. Barely five years old, and I guarantee he'll win. I wish his grandpa had lived to see it."

He'd forgotten about riding that sheep. It had been the summer he'd competed in his first rodeo. And he'd been proud to wear the Western shirt Nana had made him. Needless to say, she'd been right. He'd won first place and gotten a big trophy with a sheep on top.

"Christy worries about him being quiet, and I told her the boy might not talk much, but he is fearless. He'll turn out to be a good, strong man."

Fearless? Him?

Ty stood abruptly and went to the door, so neither of them would see his emotions. Fritz let out a yip. With his heart in his throat, Ty went over to the bed and picked up the dog. "I'll bring him right back." The words came out strangled. He couldn't help it. Carried Fritz against his chest out to the hall. Fritz licked his forearm as he tried to get himself under control.

Nana thought he was fearless. She thought he'd turn out to be a good, strong man.

Maybe as a kid he'd been fearless, but now?

Tears threatened, and he squeezed his eyes shut.

A good, strong man. He scoffed. Try a closed-off loner

who couldn't even bring himself to give a short speech at the fundraiser he was hosting in honor of the love of his life.

Zoey's face didn't come to mind.

Ashlinn's did.

And that made it all worse.

Fritz licked his arm again and again. He kept the dog close, dropping a kiss on the top of his little head. Ashlinn had been right—the dog knew how to comfort him.

"Everything okay?" Cade stepped into the hall.

"I'm fine." He set Fritz on the floor. "The mutton bustin' contest brought back memories."

"Yeah, I remember being jealous of your trophy. I was too old to compete and too young for any of the other events. You'd have clung to that sheep all the way to Texas if necessary."

He stretched his neck side to side. Why was he so emotional about a good memory?

"She's right, you know." Cade's voice had a far-off quality. "You're fearless. You're a good, strong man."

"Me?" He shook his head. "No, that describes you."

"Duh. I know." He grinned, clamping his hand on Ty's shoulder. "Of course I'm a good, strong man. You are, too."

"Modest as always."

"Come on. Let's go back in there."

"You go on ahead. I—I have something I need to do. I've got to pay someone a visit."

His brother's eyes questioned him, then he nodded. Ty led Fritz down the hall. Charlene wasn't at the desk—a mercy—and he turned the corner and strode straight out the door to his truck. Blasting the AC, he backed out of the spot and drove through town to the cemetery near the banks of Jewel River. After parking, he led Fritz down the lane to the row of headstones where they'd laid family members to rest.

He stopped at the one marked Peter Moulten. He'd helped Mom pick out Dad's headstone. One corner had a flying eagle etched into it. The opposite corner featured a horse against a mountain backdrop.

Seemed like a lifetime ago they'd stood at this spot. Cade on one side of Mom, and him on the other. Cade had been living in New York City, and after the funeral had moved back to Jewel River permanently. In the years his brother had been away, Ty had grown even closer to their father. Losing him had been devastating.

Fritz stuck his nose in the flowers his mom had planted. Ty looked around to make sure no one else was about. He had the cemetery to himself.

"I miss you, Dad." He dropped to one knee and took off his cowboy hat. "I wish you were here to give me some advice."

His father had never been one to tell him what to do unless he was clearly in the wrong, and then his dad had plenty to say. Ty had hung on his every word, good or bad.

"This is harder than I expected." The man would tell him to be more specific. He struggled to put his feelings into words. "I don't know. I miss you. I could use your wisdom right now. About Ashlinn. Nana. Zoey. All of them. I know Cade's right about me giving a short speech. I don't want to do it. I don't want to stand up there and have everyone staring at me."

It would only take a few minutes, then Cade would handle the rest. What was really bothering him?

"The whole point of planning the fundraiser was to honor Zoey's memory. And I'm a hypocrite. I said I'd love her forever, yet here I am—drawn to Ashlinn. Everyone will see me up there talking about Zoey, and they'll know I'm falling for someone else. How can I ask them to donate to a cause in her memory when I'm not keeping her memory the way I should?"

And there it was. The thing he'd been fighting.

He'd believed he'd never get over Zoey. And he'd broken his own promise.

Even if he ended up being alone forever, he couldn't pretend he hadn't moved on.

"I'm sorry, Dad. I'm not the man you raised me to be."

A blast of wind cooled his neck, and he pushed against his knee to stand. Fritz danced at his feet, waiting to be picked up. Ty lifted him into his arms.

The event was in exactly two weeks. He couldn't call it off because he felt guilty. Too many people had put a lot of time and effort into it. Erica, Mom, Charlene, Cade. And, of course, Ashlinn. Not to mention, Patrick was relying on using the money they raised to buy a van.

Ty had already let himself down. He couldn't let all of them down, too.

He knew what he had to do. But he didn't want to do it.

He needed to prepare a speech for the event.

And it was time to call Zoey's parents.

God, I'm not ready.

He wished he could discuss all this with Ashlinn. He appreciated her insightful thoughts. But how could he? It wouldn't be fair to her.

Neither of them could handle forever. Why complicate things more than they already were?

Chapter Ten

"**I**'ll be fine." Ashlinn tried to reassure Ty with a smile the following Thursday afternoon. "I want to tour the Winston with you. We need to figure out the layout—where to have all the tables set up for people to eat. Plus the food, desserts— all of it. We'll also need a few long tables for the silent auction items."

"I can probably do it myself." He rubbed the back of his neck, tipping his cowboy hat in the process. "Maybe."

"I know you can figure it out, but I want to be with you." She shoved her bare feet into sandals and grabbed Peanut's harness from the basket. "We only have one week left."

"Erica can give me tips."

Ashlinn frowned. Why was he pushing back on this when he'd been the one to ask her if she wanted to join him today?

"If you don't want me there, say the word." She put her hands on her hips, all too aware that if she got worked up, she'd be getting a stare-down from Peanut soon.

"I want you there." His imploring eyes spoke the truth. So, what was his problem? "I don't want to push you. You've only been out to my ranch and to the park. I want you to feel safe and comfortable."

She relaxed. He wasn't trying to push her away. He was looking out for her. As usual.

"No one will be around besides Erica to see me faint if it comes to that. I should be okay. Let's go."

Ty went to her kitchen and came back with a bag of potato chips. Stowed them in the tote bag next to the front door. She jiggled her tumbler. Full enough. Ty helped Peanut into the harness as Fritz trotted from her to Peanut to Ty, clearly excited about whatever was happening.

Soon, they were driving past endless prairies. Cattle and the occasional stand of trees broke up the landscape, and blue sky met mountains in the distance.

"It's beautiful."

"I agree." He glanced at her with an intensity that made her skin flush. Was he talking about the landscape...or about her?

They'd gotten together twice this week, but Ty had been quieter than usual. Something had been on his mind. Still was, as far as she could tell. And he didn't seem to want to share it.

"You called the caterer with the final head count?" she asked.

"Yes."

"And your mom's collecting the final auction items?"

"Most people dropped them off to her house. Clem drove her around to pick up the others. When I stopped by yesterday, I couldn't believe how much everyone had donated. There has to be over fifty baskets full of stuff."

"People around here sure are generous. This is for such a great cause."

She sensed him stiffen. Now what had she said?

"What are you going to wear?" she asked.

"My best Western shirt. Dress jeans. Cowboy boots. What about you?"

"Me?" She was taken aback. "I'm not going." Did he honestly think she'd be attending?

"You have to go with me." He gave her a sideways glance. "I want everyone to know how much work you put into it. They'll be able to see for themselves how important service dogs are to their owners."

Disappointment slammed into her. Her hopes had soared at the words *with me*. She'd thought he meant as a date. But he didn't. He wanted to share the credit with her. Wanted everyone to see her with her service dog.

He had a point about letting people see Peanut. What if she fainted, though? What if she got sick? She couldn't exactly set up a fainting station in the middle of a crowded banquet floor.

"It might help people to see Peanut," she said softly. "But I don't need any credit for the event. I barely helped."

"That's not true. You designed the flyers and the social media stuff. I never would have known what to do about tablecloths and centerpieces and music."

"You'd have figured it out."

"No. I needed you."

He'd needed her. Past tense. This conversation was killing her. If she'd had any illusions about Ty changing his mind about dating or marriage, she no longer did. She'd pretend they were just friends, and maybe her heart would believe it. He'd been honest with her from day one.

"Have you written what you're going to say?" He'd told her about Cade suggesting he welcome everyone, to tell them about Zoey and to highlight Howard Service Dogs. Ashlinn had assured him it was a good idea.

"Um, I'm still working on it." He tapped his fingertips against the steering wheel.

"What's wrong?" she asked.

"Nothing." The tapping stopped. "I don't want to pressure you, but I really want you to go to the event. I know I'm asking a lot, but I talked to Erica. She said they have empty rooms used by bridal parties. I figure we could set up a fainting station in one of them. Peanut will be by your side. I will, too, except for the speech. What do you think? Will you be my date?"

Her pulse took off faster than a lightning bolt. His date. Ty Moulten's guest. Hadn't she been dreaming about dating him for weeks?

But were they just friends? Or more? Was God answering her prayer? Or was she hoping for something not meant for her?

She was so confused.

Her parents had warned her not to get too close to him. He'd warned her himself that he didn't see marriage in his future—he'd already loved Zoey and wasn't falling in love again.

But maybe…they could have one date. She could wear a pretty dress. The one in her closet she'd never had a chance to wear before. With Peanut by her side and a special room where she could go if her blood pressure took a dive…

"Yes, I'll be your date." Her fears skyrocketed as soon as the words left her mouth. She should have taken some time to think about it. Should have weighed the pros and cons. Probably should have prayed about it first.

He took her hand and squeezed. "Thank you."

Pros. Cons. Who cared? Ty was holding her hand. Whatever happened would be worth it.

They listened to the radio, and Ashlinn admired the open land before her. She hadn't seen much of Wyoming, and the bareness of it spoke to her soul. Out here everything had room to breathe. Including her.

They arrived at Winston Ranch, and Ty parked in front of a large pole barn with fancy doors. Erica greeted them inside.

"Hey, Ty, glad you could make it." The woman smiled broadly, shook his hand and turned to Ashlinn. "And you must be Ashlinn. I've heard so much about you. I'm sorry I didn't get a chance to meet you at the movie in the park. I'm Erica Cambridge."

"You were in charge of the event—no need to apologize." Ashlinn shook her hand. "It's nice to meet you."

"You brought Fritz." Erica crouched to pet the dog, then rose and nodded to Peanut. "And who is this handsome fellow?"

"Peanut." Ashlinn kept a tight grip on the harness's handle. "He's my service dog."

"I love golden retrievers. I mean, look at that happy face. I'd spoil him rotten." Erica pointed to the large open area. "Come on. I'll give you a tour."

Ty held up Ashlinn's tote. "Mind if we see one of those rooms first? Just in case?"

"Of course." She waved for them to follow her. "This way."

Erica led them to a hallway, then strode briskly past restrooms to a door. She opened it for them to enter and switched on the lights. Ashlinn made note of how far the room was from the banquet hall. If she was attending this dinner, she needed to make sure her table was close by.

The first thing that came to mind as she took in the room was rustic chic. Twinkling chandeliers overhead made the room bright. Two large area rugs covered the hardwood floors, and couches and overstuffed chairs were arranged around coffee tables to make two seating areas. A counter lined a portion of the far wall. Stools and light-up mirrors had been stationed along the counter for bridesmaids to get ready.

Ashlinn closed her eyes briefly. *I want to get married and have my reception here.*

But she wasn't getting married.

The thought lodged like a stone in her heart. What would it be like to have a room full of bridesmaids getting ready at those mirrors?

"If you need to come in here at any time, the room will be all yours." Erica placed her hand on Ashlinn's arm, and she fought the urge to cover it with her own hand. Erica's generosity, caring nature and overall enthusiasm added up to one impressive woman.

"Okay if I leave this here for now, Ash?" Ty motioned to the tote he set near one of the couches.

"Yes."

Fritz sniffed around and returned to Ty's side.

"Let me grab my tablet, and we'll do a walk-through. You can let me know how you want everything set up. Give me one sec." Erica held up an index finger and left the room.

"You doing okay?" Ty took her free hand in his, looking into her eyes.

"I'm okay." She was perplexed by this new desire for a wedding. It seemed the more time she spent with Ty, the more she wanted things she couldn't have.

Her parents had definitely been right to warn her to guard her heart.

"Here. Want a drink?" He handed her the tumbler of water.

"Thanks." She took a drink, spilling a few drops on her shirt. Trying to lighten the mood, she glanced down, then met Ty's eyes. "Can't take me anywhere."

"I disagree." His lazy smile made her heart thump.

Erica popped her head through the doorway. "Are you ready?"

He arched his eyebrows to Ashlinn, and she nodded. The

sooner she left this room, the sooner she could stop thinking about weddings. She and Peanut joined Erica in the hallway with Ty and Fritz behind them.

In the main area, Erica swiped her tablet. "Okay, Ty, we're doing round tables, correct?"

"Yes."

"White tablecloths. You'll have the centerpieces. Will you provide a program for each place setting?"

He glanced at Ashlinn. She nodded. "Yes, they should be arriving by Wednesday."

She and Ty had put the program together and, after some back-and-forth, had agreed on the colors and layout.

"How will the tables be set up?" Ty asked.

"See up there?" Erica pointed to the kitchen. "The food will be in warming trays on the counters for a buffet-style meal. And over there—" she gestured to a large open space near the kitchen "—will be the drink station."

Ashlinn could picture it all.

"The podium and microphone will be set up on a platform here." Erica pointed behind them. "It's the best location for everyone to see you, plus it's tucked against the wall."

"I'll only be up there for a minute," Ty said. "Cade's doing most of the talking."

"That's fine." Erica nodded. "So the tables will be in this area." She made a circling motion with her hand. "I was thinking the silent auction would work in the far corner."

Ty and Ashlinn turned to where she indicated.

"What do you think?" Erica asked.

"Against the wall?" Ashlinn brought her finger to her chin. "Or will guests be able to walk on either side?"

"It depends. How many tables will you need?"

Ty shrugged. "I'm not sure. Mom has everything at her place. There are a lot of donations."

"What if we set up a few rows? That way people will have room to stroll around and see everything?"

"I like the idea," Ashlinn said. "Three long tables in each row, and two long tables against the wall to make it shaped like a U."

"That should work perfectly." Erica tapped out a note on the tablet. "What about sign-up sheets for the auction items?" They discussed trivial matters, went over the timeline and when the hall would be available to bring in everything.

"Now, Ty." Erica grew serious. "What about Zoey?"

Ashlinn halted. Zoey? The name was like a knife to her heart.

"I'm not following." Ty looked down at Fritz, standing near his feet.

"Are you going to have a display with photographs? Something you'll need an easel for? Or do you want a small table? We can cover it with a tablecloth and put a framed picture of her on it."

He wiped his palm down his cheek. "I don't know."

"I thought since you wanted the dinner to be in her memory, you'd have something to commemorate her with. It would help the people who didn't know her well put a face with her name."

"Yeah, that makes sense." His cheeks had lost a shade of color. Fritz let out a yip and danced at his feet. He picked up the dog and petted him absentmindedly.

"Let me know what you come up with. I'll save a spot near the entrance for people to see when they arrive."

He nodded, and Ashlinn noted Fritz licking his arm. Ty was stressed. And so was she.

Peanut licked her hand. "Okay, buddy. Ty? I'm going to the bridal room."

"I'll come with you."

"I think we've covered everything. Let yourselves out whenever you're ready." Erica gave them both a smile. "Call me if you need anything else."

Ty and Ashlinn made their way in silence to the room. She lowered herself to one of the area rugs and told Peanut to cover her thighs. Ty handed her the tumbler, and he sat on one of the couches with Fritz on his lap.

The past hour had cemented a few things in her mind. This event was sure to be a special night. And she regretted agreeing to be Ty's date.

The night would only remind him of Zoey and everything he'd lost. It would solidify his stance on remaining single.

Even if she was wrong, it wouldn't matter. She'd be flat on her back in a bridal suite meant for other people, not for her. Or she'd be sitting at a table, listening to stories about Zoey and how tragic it was that Ty had lost the love of his life.

No matter what, she'd be faced with the truth. Neither she nor Ty had the emotional tools necessary to move forward. She had no future with Ty Moulten, and she'd better get used to it.

Maybe his mom would know what to do.

Ty had spent the past two days pushing away thoughts of Zoey and the fundraiser. He still hadn't reached out to her parents, and he couldn't bring himself to go through the box of Zoey's items he'd stored in his closet.

He'd removed all the photos of Zoey from his phone years ago. For months after her death, he'd been stuck in a loop of scrolling through them throughout the day. He'd finally had to limit his access to them by storing them all on a flash drive. He wasn't sure he was ready to open the flash drive again and see her smiling face or remember all he'd lost.

It seemed particularly foolish at the moment. He was finally opening up to someone other than his mom or brother. Ashlinn had become important to him, and he hadn't talked to her since dropping her off Thursday evening. She'd been quiet all the way home. He'd assumed the Winston tour had tired her out. But now he wasn't sure. Maybe she was avoiding him.

Her replies to his texts had been emojis or one or two words. Not like her. He'd asked if she was feeling okay, and she'd assured him she was.

Maybe he should stop by her place. Check on her. No, Ashlinn clearly needed some space, and he knew all about needing space.

After parking on the street in front of his mother's house, he loped up the driveway and knocked on the door. She opened it and drew him in for a hug. Tulip sniffed his cowboy boots, and Ty picked her up to pet her.

"Want a glass of iced tea?" His mother retreated down the hall.

"No, thanks."

"Coffee? Cookie?"

"I'm fine, Ma." He made himself comfortable on her couch, and Tulip jumped down.

"How's Ashlinn?" Mom asked, sitting on her favorite chair and placing Tulip on her lap.

"Good." He hoped so, at least. What if she was going through a flare-up? Did she need supplies? Maybe he *should* have stopped by.

"Is she going to the fundraiser?"

"Yes. I asked her to join me." He prepared himself for his mother's reaction. Her eyebrows rose, and her lips formed an O. "But that's not why I'm here."

Her face fell. "What's wrong?"

"I need some advice."

"From me?" She placed her palm against her chest.

"Yes. Erica thinks I should have a small table near the entrance with pictures of Zoey."

His mom tapped her chin. "Smart thinking. A framed photo would be lovely. Or we could create a collage. Set it up behind the table. Yes." She nodded to herself. "Erica doesn't miss a beat."

"I don't know."

"About what?"

"I feel funny about it."

"Honey, you're hosting this dinner in honor of her. Don't you think a few pictures would be appropriate?"

"I'm sure they would be. But I don't want to pick them out. I'm not even sure I can face her."

"Her?" She scoffed, petting the dog. "Don't you mean a photograph?"

"Yes." The word came out harsh. They were one and the same in his mind.

"Why?" Her expression was genuinely confused.

Now he had to explain himself. Bile rose in his throat. "I thought I'd never get over her. And we're hosting this dinner, and I—" He couldn't say it out loud.

"You're over her," she said quietly.

He nodded, shame crushing him.

"You're afraid of being a hypocrite. Going to all these lengths to honor her memory when you're not mourning her anymore."

How his mother had gotten so smart he'd never know.

"The two things can coexist, you know."

"How?"

"You can honor her memory without pining for her. You can move on with your life and still regret she's no longer in it. It's not paralyzing you anymore. That's a good thing."

"It doesn't feel good."

"Only because it's new."

"So you're saying I should bring pictures? Have them framed or something?"

"Yes. You aren't the only one who loved her, you know. She had a lot of friends in this town. They'll want to see her face again, and they'll also be glad that you're honoring her memory."

"What if they aren't glad? What if they realize I'm not the guy they thought I was?"

"How many of them have you talked to in the past six years?" She was treating him gently, and for that he was thankful.

"None."

"Then you couldn't possibly know what any of them think of you. If they're like most people, they'll want to see you move on with your life."

He massaged the back of his neck. "Move on? Zoey died. Her life was cut short. What gives me the right to be happy and have a life?"

"Is that what you think? That you need to hide away because your fiancée died a long time ago? Life goes on. You might not like it, but it keeps moving no matter what. You need to keep living."

"I've been living."

"Have you? I mean, I guess it's true. Somewhat." Her tone warned him she was wrestling with how much to say. "Until recently, you haven't been enjoying life, though. It's okay to enjoy it, Ty."

He shook his head.

"I lost your dad and thought I'd never be happy again." She stared down at the fluffball on her lap. "Around six months after he died, I forced myself to have lunch with my friends. We made it a weekly date. As time wore on, I got back to living. I found myself smiling again. I'd feel guilty about it—like how can I enjoy anything without Pete here?"

"That's different," he said gruffly. He wasn't sure how it was different, though.

"Maybe. Maybe not. I made a choice. To live. To enjoy life. I still miss your father. Oh, boy, do I miss him. But I don't think anyone, especially you boys, wanted me to fall apart and be miserable the rest of my life."

"Of course we don't."

"My situation was different, though. And I'm different. You're introverted and needed to stay home. I like being around people. Depression can put a damper on life."

"Who said anything about depression?" He'd never been diagnosed, but then, he'd never gone to a doctor, either.

"Ty, the signs were there. I tried to help."

For years she'd hounded him about seeing a doctor. Seemed like every other month, she was calling or texting him about it. He'd ignored her.

"I don't know what's going on in your head right now, but I think hosting this fundraiser, adopting Fritz and getting close to Ashlinn have all forced you to do things out of your comfort zone. You're changing, and change can be scary."

He pondered her words for a few moments. "You make it look easy. Grieving. Getting back to life."

"Me?" She half snorted, half laughed. "No. It's not easy. I pray each morning for guidance, for discernment. And I think more changes are coming for me."

"What do you mean?" He didn't like the sound of that.

"Believe it or not, I've been getting close to Clem."

"Clem Buckley?" He couldn't wrap his head around what she was saying. Sure, Clem had been acting as her unofficial driver after his attempts at improving her driving skills had failed. But getting close? To steely-eyed Clem?

"Yes." A soft smile played on her lips. "I know it's strange. I never in a million years would have thought… Never mind. You didn't come here to discuss me. What can I do to help you finalize the fundraiser?"

"Oh, no, you don't. You can't toss out Clem's name and change the subject." He stood and began to pace. "Are you two dating?"

"No. I mean, obviously, he drives me around. All of his attempts at teaching me road etiquette have failed. I've pretty much accepted the fact I'll never be able to keep my license. But he doesn't mind driving me. In fact, I think he prefers it when he's behind the wheel and I'm the passenger."

"But that's just being friendly, right?" He couldn't fathom anything beyond that at this point.

"It started out that way. But we've also been spending time doing fun things together. Like last week, he took me fishing on his property. I didn't catch a thing. I got to wear waders, though, and that was fun. And the week before that, I made him drive me to Buffalo, and he didn't hate the artsy stores we visited. He even bought a handcrafted mug with a horseshoe on it."

"I'm surprised you haven't killed each other by now." What else didn't he know about his mother?

"Shocking, I know. And yes, we're both still alive. I like that I can argue with him. He speaks what's on his mind. There are no misunderstandings."

Ty thought of Ashlinn. Up until Thursday, he'd have said the same about her. But now? He definitely needed to get to the bottom of what was wrong.

"Don't go thinking we're getting married or anything."

Fear and excitement mingled in his mom's eyes. "I'm growing close to him, that's all."

"Married?" Now, that was crossing a line. Or was it? He studied his mom and noted how time had been changing her. More wrinkles, more joy in her wise face. She was beautiful—inside and out.

"Don't ask me to call Clem Dad," he said with a straight face to see how she'd react.

"Ty! No one is calling anyone dad." She shook her head with a huff. "My word. You'd think I'd announced an engagement."

"Calm down. I'm just teasing you."

She threw a pillow at him. It bounced off his head. He laughed. Hadn't seen her this riled up in a while.

"Does Cade know about this?" he asked.

"I haven't told him."

"Are you going to?"

She sighed. "Yes. When the time is right."

"Wish I could see the look on his face when you do." He went over and hugged her. "You could do worse than Clem."

"You think so?" Her vulnerability touched him.

"Clem's a stand-up guy. Kind of scary, too. But someone you can depend on." He stepped back. "I'm going to take off. I've got some pictures to go through."

"If you need moral support..."

"I'll be okay." He sounded confident, but he wasn't.

"Oh, and tell Ashlinn if she needs any help getting ready—her hair, nails, that sort of thing—I'd be tickled pink to come over." Mom tucked Tulip under her arm as she got up.

From Zoey to Ashlinn. Ty was pretty sure he'd gotten whiplash. "Why don't you tell her? You've got her number."

"You don't think she'd mind?"

"No. I think she'd appreciate it."

"I will." She beamed.

And on that note, he prepared to make his escape. "I'm going to take off."

She walked him to the door, and he hugged her again. All the way to his truck, his resolve hardened. He was checking on Ashlinn. And after he verified she was okay, he needed to give himself a pep talk to get the courage to call Zoey's parents. As for going through her pictures, he wasn't ready. He hoped he wouldn't fall apart when the time came to do it.

Chapter Eleven

Ashlinn couldn't think of a more miserable Saturday than this one. Oh, the weather was fine. The problem was her. She was a nervous wreck and probably would be passing out soon. She'd been blowing off Ty's texts since Thursday, and while she felt horrible for doing it, she didn't have much choice.

She could *not* be his date to the fundraiser.

And she needed to break the news to him soon.

Was it smart to be tying herself into knots over how to tell him? She hated breaking her word and letting him down. Had she built up what they had to be something more than what it was?

Peanut had been staring at her for over a minute. She was sitting on the floor with her back against the couch. Blood pressure monitor on. Weighted blanket over her legs.

She'd been in a constant state of anxiety for the past two days.

Not good.

Her stress levels were too high, and if she wasn't careful, she'd pay the price with a flare-up like she'd had when she couldn't keep food down a few weeks ago.

What if her health reverted to something worse? The fear of being bedridden for months on end filled her mind.

A knock on the door made her groan. It could only be Patrick, Mackenzie or Ty, and Patrick had already checked on her today, so Mackenzie wouldn't. That left Ty.

With slow, deliberate moves, she hauled herself up to a standing position. Then she shuffled to the door, opened it and immediately turned to resume her position on the floor.

"Hey, are you all right?" Ty closed the door and followed her to the couch.

"I'm good." She was far from good, but what else could she say? That she was falling so hard for him she thought she might shatter? That he clearly still loved a dead woman, and he'd been honest with her about it, but she'd ignored it?

"You don't look good."

"Thanks a lot," she said under her breath.

"Sorry. That's not what I meant."

"I know." She took a drink of water. Wished he'd leave. Wanted him to stay.

"What's been going on? Your texts have been...short."

"Oh?" Her chest tightened. She wasn't ready for this conversation. Not on the floor. Not when she was about to pass out.

"I'm worried about you."

"You sound like my mother." She shouldn't accuse him of that—it wasn't fair to him.

He plunked down on the floor, sitting directly in front of her with Peanut lying at her side.

"I'm sorry for being nosy, Ash. I...care about you."

"I appreciate it." She met his eyes then. Big mistake. Because he did care about her. "I'm fine. Really. Nothing I can't handle."

"Why don't I make supper?" he asked. "It's a little early, but I can put together sandwiches."

Oh, how she wanted this to last. She liked having supper

with him. Loved when he made something simple for them to eat and they'd talk about their days.

"I've got plans."

The way he was blinking, she'd surprised him.

"What plans?" His tone was guarded.

Why was she dragging this out? He'd done her a favor by coming over here. Now she could tell him in person.

"I'm not going to the fundraiser with you, Ty." The words pierced the air between them, leaving her relieved and disappointed.

"You really aren't feeling good, are you?"

"It has nothing to do with my health."

"Then why?"

She stroked Peanut's fur, thankful he wasn't alerting her. She might be able to get everything she needed to say out before she fainted.

"I don't want to mislead you. You were quite clear when we met that you'd already lost someone you'd loved and you're not getting married or having kids. I've been conveniently forgetting that—or ignoring it—I'm not sure. At the Winston it sank in that you'd spoken the truth."

"I meant what I'd said when we met." The words came out so quiet she almost missed them. "But I don't know anymore."

"I like you, Ty, I like you a lot. But this—" she gestured to the dog, to the cuff on his wrist, to the tumbler "—is my life. It's not likely to get better from here on out, and it could get worse. Much worse."

He shifted his jaw. "You told me what you have isn't fatal."

"It's not. I'll live with the disease and manage it as best I can until I grow old."

"Then what's the problem?"

She could see it clearly now. The way he fussed over her

and cared for her? She'd put him in the same position as she'd put her parents. He felt responsible for her, and it wasn't fair to him. "I'm someone to take care of. Not a partner to spend your life with."

"What does this have to do with the fundraiser?" His face grew hard. "We're talking about one date. To an event we both planned. No one said anything about forever."

Maybe that was the problem. She wanted forever. One date wouldn't be enough. She'd want another and another...

"I'm sorry, Ty. I'm not going."

His face clouded over, and she held her breath, waiting for him to argue. Peanut licked her hand, and she tried to breathe normally.

"Maybe we're both scared, Ash." He stood up. "I'm going to sit in that chair until Peanut stops alerting you. And I'm asking you to keep an open mind. On Thursday, if you still don't want to come with me, I'll accept it. Fair?"

None of this was fair. She'd told him she wasn't going. But a part of her clung to the idea of having a few more days to decide.

"I'm not going to change my mind."

"Then you can turn me down again when I stop by on Thursday."

"Don't come over Thursday." Why couldn't he accept what she was saying? "I've gotten too close to you. Maybe it was inevitable. I've been isolated for six years. And here you are—this kind, amazing cowboy. Who wouldn't fall for you? I never should have gotten close. I'm sorry. But I can't be your date now or ever."

"You're falling for me?"

Leave it to him to latch on to the one thing she shouldn't have admitted.

She nodded, dangerously close to tears.

"I'm falling for you, too."

"Fall for someone else. All I do is faint or get sick and have to stay in bed. You lost Zoey. You deserve someone who can love you well. Someone who doesn't need a service dog to get through life. Someone who won't embarrass you when you go out."

"You could never embarrass me." His face gave nothing away. Not relief, not pain.

"*I* embarrass me. Okay? And I'm not going to be your burden. Find someone who can ride horses around your ranch and give you ten babies and fly to a tropical island for your honeymoon. I want you to have a full life, and you won't with me."

Exhaustion and mortification sapped her energy. Why had she blabbed on as if he'd proposed?

"I'm fine riding solo around the ranch." He started to rise. "I never thought I'd have babies—even with Zoey. And I'm not a tropical island kind of guy. But I can see you're not in a state to talk. I don't want to rile you up. But I *will* be back Thursday afternoon, and you can tell me to my face if you're still not coming with me. I'll leave you alone after that. You have my word."

"You're never going to be over her." She hadn't meant to say it.

The color drained from his face.

She looked away, closed her eyes tightly, willing him to leave. She wanted to shout at him to get out of there. But he didn't deserve that—didn't deserve any of what she'd just said. She'd spewed out way too much and hurt his feelings. Her lungs felt like two rocks in her chest.

She couldn't have Ty Moulten. She never should have pretended otherwise.

* * *

Nothing was going right today. Two hours later, Ty sat on his couch and stared at the phone in his hand. Fritz had claimed his lap and was softly snoring.

Every time he thought of Ashlinn, he forced his attention elsewhere. Had briefly considered saddling up and riding around the ranch. It was how he'd gotten through life after Zoey died. But something had stopped him.

He needed to sit with this. To deal with it.

And he didn't want to.

He hung his head and closed his eyes.

God, I don't know what to do.

Ashlinn was right. He'd told her he wasn't getting married or having kids. He'd grown close to her—not just as friends. She'd admitted she was falling for him. Was she? Really?

From the minute they'd met, he'd known he couldn't offer her his heart. At the time, he'd thought it was because he didn't have one to offer. But now? His heart had been healing. Would always be scarred. He didn't know if he was brave enough to risk having it broken again.

Six years of riding around his ranch, avoiding anything that required the most basic interaction with people around town. Six years of numbness and misery and convincing himself it was the way it had to be.

Six years.

Wasn't it about time to get out of this limbo? Was he going to live in a state of nothingness forever?

He glanced at his phone, swiped it and found the contact he'd been avoiding. Pressed it. And waited. His pulse throbbed in his neck.

"Hello?"

"Hi, Mrs. Daniels. It's Ty Moulten." His throat clogged with fear. Would she be upset with him for not keeping in touch? Would this call cause her pain? Remind her of losing their daughter? He didn't want to hurt her any more than she'd already suffered. Maybe calling was a mistake.

"Ty!" The surprise in her tone was upbeat. "How are you? It's been a long time—I hope you're doing well."

It *had* been a long time. Her voice triggered so many emotions and memories. She'd been kind to him. Zoey's dad, Mike, had, too. They'd treated him like a son. And how had he repaid them? With silence.

"I am. And you?" He couldn't get out any more words. Guilt and sadness choked him.

"Doing just fine." Did he detect a trace of wistfulness in her tone? "Rob got married a few years ago, and we found out they're expecting another baby."

Rob was married? He remembered him being fresh out of high school. "Congratulations. You're a grandma now, huh?"

"And proud of it. Trinity just turned eighteen months. She's a busy girl. I quit my job at the bank to babysit her while they work. Best decision I ever made." She went on to tell him that Mike planned on retiring in ten years. A sense of incredulity mounted as she talked.

Mr. and Mrs. Daniels were doing okay. They didn't seem to be pining for their loss.

What had he expected? Tears? A guilt trip for not staying in touch with them? Mournful reminiscences of Zoey?

"Listen to me going on and on. I'm sorry, Ty. Tell me about yourself. How are you getting on?" Her cheery voice only highlighted the difference between them. She was busy living. And he wasn't. Just like his mom had said.

"Doing okay." He tried to keep it light. "Still ranching."

"Of course you are. Born in a saddle—that's what I always told Mike."

He chuckled out of politeness. "That's me. I adopted a dog recently. He's a fun little guy."

"Good for you."

"In fact, I adopted him from a local trainer. He opened Howard Service Dogs in Jewel River, and I'm hosting a fundraising dinner this Friday night. It's in Zoey's honor, and all the proceeds are going to the training center. I'm sorry I didn't tell you about it sooner. I just... I don't know."

"What a thoughtful thing to do." She went from happy to somber. "You're the son-in-law I always wanted. I hate that Zoey died before you two could get married. And I'm sorry we moved away and didn't keep up with you."

"*You're* sorry?" It didn't make sense. "I should be apologizing to you. I could have called. At least sent a Christmas card or something."

"It was hard. Too hard." Her voice sounded a million miles away. "For all of us."

"Yes." The emotions roared back—this time bringing tears to the backs of his eyes. "There isn't a day I don't think about her. I loved her."

"I know. We all know. It was never in question."

Neither spoke for a while. He sensed they both needed space to work through their feelings.

"Ty, I hope you find someone to share your life with. Maybe you already have. If not, though, open your heart. You'll see Zoey again in the next life. Until then, make the most of the one you've got."

They spoke for a few more minutes and ended the call.

Ty's head reeled. Mrs. Daniels had told him to move on and make the most of his life. To open his heart. And she'd meant it.

From all appearances, their family *had* moved on.

He placed Fritz on the floor and stood, pocketing his phone. An irrational tension hummed through his body.

In the mudroom, he swiped his cowboy hat off the hook and planted in on his head. Then he shoved his feet into cowboy boots and went outside, slamming the door behind him. His pace quickened as he approached the stables.

Everyone was moving on.

Mom had created a new life without Dad as if their years together had never happened. When she'd mentioned having feelings for Clem, it hadn't bothered him much, but the more he thought about it? Yuck.

And then there was the Daniels family. By all accounts living their best lives in another state as if their years in Wyoming—and the life they'd had with their daughter—had never happened. Like she'd never mattered.

Zoey had happened. She'd mattered.

She'd been the sweetest person he'd ever met. She'd gotten him. Liked things simple—the same as he did.

He'd loved her so much. And she'd died anyway.

Why had she died? And why had everyone moved on?

He went straight to the tack room, grabbed everything he needed and got his horse from the paddock. Methodically saddled it and hoisted himself up. Didn't take long to reach the lane leading to the creek, where he nudged the horse to go faster, concentrating on the wind blowing against his face and the thud of the hooves on the ground.

"You're never going to be over her." Ashlinn's voice cut through the jumbled thoughts in his head.

He'd gotten over Zoey. But he'd promised he never would.

"I'm the only one who refuses to forget her," he yelled to the air. "I loved her. I love her. What am I supposed to do? It's not fair. It was never fair!"

The horse galloped along the creek until he slowed the horse to a trot, then a walk.

A red-tailed hawk soared overhead in the blue sky. The subtle change in the temperature told him summer was ending. Autumn would be in full swing soon. He could make out pops of yellow and red in the trees up ahead.

He dismounted. Took a stone from the water and let the coolness of it seep into his palm, then clenched his fist around it. Couldn't believe he'd gotten himself into this situation. He never should have spent so much time with Ashlinn.

If Zoey could see him now...

She'd be hurt. Stunned. Disappointed. Shocked he'd gotten close to another woman after the promises he'd made her.

She'd be...

He stared off toward the horizon.

Dead.

Still dead. Always dead. That part never went away.

The future he and Zoey had planned in those weeks before she'd gotten sick and died would never happen. She'd sat in his arms on his couch and dreamed about their life after marriage.

"We'll have a boy and a girl. Two dogs. And a screened-in porch. I've always wanted one of those." She'd shifted to smile up at him.

"A screened-in porch, huh? I can start building one. The kids will have to wait until after we're married, though." He'd kissed the top of her head, pained to play pretend. Zoey wasn't ever having kids. They'd both known it. "You can pick out the dogs anytime."

The stone fell out of his hand and rolled to a stop in the prairie grass at the edge of the creek. He took off his cowboy hat, letting it dangle near his thigh, and stared ahead at the land.

He hadn't been able to save her. His love hadn't been enough. He'd never thought she'd die before the wedding. Had always assumed they'd have a couple of years together. That, at the very least, he'd have time to build her that screened-in porch.

"God, can't You rewind it? Make it all make sense?" Tears flowed down his cheeks. He raised his face and shook his fist to the sky. "I'll always love you, Zoey Daniels!"

His hand fell, his shoulders shook, and he took big, gulping breaths. He wiped his face with the handkerchief from his back pocket.

"But I'm not in love with you anymore," he whispered.

It had happened over time. He hadn't realized he was moving on. He should have tried harder to prevent it.

For reasons he didn't want to examine, confessing everything out loud in the Wyoming air was necessary. Felt right. "The truth is—and it seems I'm spilling everything today, even the things I won't admit to myself—I'm in love with someone else. And I'm sorry about that, Zoey. I don't expect you to forgive me."

Could he forgive himself?

"I failed you. I didn't keep my promise. And I'm sorry."

When the sun began to set, he got back in the saddle and took his time returning to the stables.

Zoey was gone.

Ashlinn didn't want him. He didn't blame her.

He'd always have the ranch, but it didn't have the same draw as it had before Ashlinn had arrived in Jewel River.

His future looked as bleak as it had since the day Zoey died. Maybe Ashlinn cutting him out of her life was for the best. Then he wouldn't have another imaginary future ripped out of his grasp.

Chapter Twelve

She'd passed out again.

Ashlinn's eyelids fluttered open. She tried to recall where she was. The living room window revealed a black sky. The television was off. Middle of the night? Peanut licked and nibbled her hand. "Good boy."

She felt around the floor until she grasped her phone. Checked the time. After midnight. She wished she had a girlfriend who was a night owl. One she could call and tell all her problems.

Lately, she had a lot of problems.

In the three days since she'd told Ty she couldn't be his date, she'd fainted over twice as many times as she typically did. The stress of pushing him away—and of him staying away—was ramping up her AAG symptoms. And this added more stress, causing her to be nauseous.

Worry was eating away at her, robbing her of her improved health.

On Sunday, she'd watched a church service on her laptop, and she'd felt so sorry for herself afterward, she'd broken down in tears. Her mom called three times a day, and every conversation was the same. How many times had she fainted? How was her stomach? Did they need to make a doctor appointment? Was she keeping her blood pressure monitor nearby?

Yesterday, Ashlinn had let all calls go to voice mail. She hadn't had it in her to go through the drill again. She'd texted her mom that she was fine, just busy.

She was neither.

She was heartbroken.

She'd told Ty she was falling for him, but she'd lied. She wasn't falling for him. She'd already gone and done it. She'd fallen for him. Past tense.

Propping herself on her elbows, she debated trying to stand to go to bed. Too soon. She'd pass out if she attempted it now. Petting Peanut, she ignored the awful ache in her chest.

Ty hadn't called or texted her. And she missed him. Missed what they'd had. She'd grown comfortable with him. Enjoyed having him around. He made her feel…normal.

She missed her mother, too—the one she'd been before Ashlinn had gotten sick. Sure, the woman had always been overprotective, but she'd also cared about Ashlinn's hopes, dreams and problems.

Ashlinn wished her mom was capable of viewing her as a mature adult instead of an invalid incapable of making a rational decision.

Had cutting off Ty's friendship been rational?

Didn't matter. She'd made her choice. There was no going back.

Peanut licked her hand. Not again. She didn't want to pass out again. The unbearableness of it all made her want to sob.

With Ty gone, her life felt empty. She closed her eyes, tired of fighting tears. Tired of second-guessing herself. Tired of fainting. Tired of resenting her mother. Tired of telling herself she was good enough to live independently and work with Patrick, but she wasn't good enough to date a kind, patient, incredibly gorgeous cowboy.

She began to shiver. Curling up on her side, she was brutally aware of the hard floor beneath the rug. All she wanted
to do was crawl into bed. But she couldn't. Because she'd
pass out before she got there.

God, I need You. I feel so low.

As she huddled there, memories chased each other in
her mind. Her first kiss—junior year in high school. They'd
dated through senior year and had gone their separate ways
after graduation. She didn't miss him. Never had. And the
friends from high school and college that she hadn't remained
close with? Not their fault. Not hers either.

But Ty…

She'd miss him. She already did.

The man wore sadness like she wore her blood pressure
cuff. Never out of reach for long.

God, I want him to smile. I want him to be happy. I want…

She wanted to be his. Forever. She wanted to live on his
pretty ranch and listen to him talk about the land and cattle.
She wanted to rock on that front porch with Fritz on her lap
and Peanut sitting next to her.

She wanted it all.

Carefully, she rose and made her way to the bedroom with
Peanut trailing her. After climbing into bed, she pulled her
Bible onto her lap and opened it to the bookmark. Romans
8:18, "For I reckon that the sufferings of this present time
are not worthy to be compared with the glory which shall
be revealed in us."

The passage gave peace to her weary soul. *God, I can trust
You. You promise that my current sufferings will end in glory.
I believe it. Help me get through this.*

She didn't feel so alone. The Bible closed, and she fell
into a restless sleep.

* * *

If one more person called needing advice on what to do for something involving the fundraiser, he was saddling his horse and riding to the next county. He wasn't meant for phone calls and decisions regarding playlists and how much ice to have on hand. The event was in two days, which meant he had to face Ashlinn tomorrow.

He wasn't looking forward to hearing her reject him all over again.

Ty tossed a bale of hay to the ground then kicked it for good measure. His phone rang. Raising his face to the barn rafters high above, he contemplated grinding the phone under his boot. He sighed. Ignoring it made more sense than totally destroying it.

Fritz trotted over from his water bowl as the phone continued to ring. Ty kicked the hay one more time.

"What did that bale do to you?" His brother's voice startled him. Earlier, Ty had opened up both sets of double doors in the barn to let the warm air circulate.

"Didn't hear you drive up." He turned back to the stack of bales, gripped the twine on one with his suede work gloves and tossed it to the ground.

"You gonna kick that one, too?" Cade bent to pick up Fritz. The dog wriggled excitedly.

"I might. Unless you want to."

"Nah. I'll leave that to you." He stroked Fritz's back as he held him. "Need any help?"

"Grab another bale." Ty nodded to the stack he was working on.

"Not with the hay. With the fundraiser. You can take care of your own cattle."

"Good, because I'd rather take care of cattle than deal with all these phone calls. I don't know why anyone thinks

I have a clue if we should have instrumental or bluegrass music playing through dinner. And I don't care if the cupcakes or the lemon bars are the first thing people see on the dessert table. What does it matter? None of it is important. People won't notice the music, and not a lick of desserts will be left by the end anyhow."

"Whoa." Cade set Fritz down. "You're worked up. Take a break. Let's go for a walk."

"Fine." He stripped off the gloves and strode to the corner where he kept supplies. Tossed them on the counter and continued outside. The sun felt good on his face. Not as hot as it had been a few weeks back. "Where to?"

"Doesn't matter to me."

"I'm thirsty. Let's grab a soda from the house. We can sit on the patio." He headed down the lane, not caring if Cade was following or not. Fritz bounded ahead of him.

"What's got you all worked up? Besides the phone calls?" Cade jogged up next to him.

"I don't want to talk about it."

"Ashlinn?"

Was he that transparent? "Zoey."

"Zoey?"

"Yeah. It feels like everyone's moved on. Like she never existed." The anger grew all over again. Why couldn't he let this go?

"Life does go on. Whether you want it to or not. Doesn't mean they don't miss her."

"I know. Do you think I don't know that?" Ty shook his head. "What do you think I've been doing all these years?"

"Whatever it was, it wasn't living."

Leave it to his brother to spit out the brutal truth. "I've been living. Working cattle, taking care of this place. What more do you want from me?"

"Let me ask you something."

He rolled his eyes, his adrenaline speeding out of control. "Go ahead."

"What do you want everyone to do? Give a speech about her at church every week? Light candles and cry at night?"

"No!"

"Dying is part of life. I hate it. I hate that you lost her. But I, for one, have been glad to see you get out more. Adopting Fritz—the dog's good for you—was a smart move. Helping Ashlinn has softened something inside you, too. So forgive me if I'm confused why you're so angry and uptight right now. I'd expect you'd be happy."

"Happy?" He stopped, turning to face Cade. "Why on earth would I be happy?"

Frowning, he tilted his head. "Why wouldn't you be? You have this ranch. Healthy cattle. A great little dog. Mom. Me. You should be grateful for me." His toothy grin didn't amuse Ty.

"I don't have Zoey. I'll never have her again." He resumed walking, and Cade did, too.

"That's right. You'll never have her. But there are people alive—here and now—who want to be with you. Mom. Mackenzie. Me. Ashlinn. Don't push us away."

"I'm not."

"You are."

The crunch of gravel under his boots couldn't drown out his brother's words.

"Seriously, Ty, I worry about you. It's taken a load off my mind to see you getting out more these past couple of months. And hosting the fundraiser? I'm proud of you, man. In fact, that's one of the reasons I came over."

"What are you talking about?"

"Mackenzie and I discussed it—we're going to match all

the donations tomorrow night. We want her dad to have that van."

The words were so unexpected, Ty rocked back on his heels. He studied Cade's face, and knew he spoke the truth. Like Cade would lie? Never.

"Really? You'd do that?" He blinked rapidly, stunned at his brother's generosity. Cade's wealth wasn't a secret or anything, but still.

"Yeah. I wish I'd thought to plan something to help him out. I'm sure it worked out better with you in charge."

"I disagree with you on that."

"I'm glad you're honoring Zoey's memory. Everyone around here is. You're not the only one who misses her, Ty. She was well liked. Her family was, too. And, believe it or not, you're well liked around here as well. I can't tell you how many people have said how nice it's been to see you around town lately."

"They're probably going to be seeing a lot less of me." He struggled to accept Cade's words.

"I hope not. I think you and Ashlinn have a good friend-ship going—"

"It's more than friendship." He ducked his chin. "I love her. I fell in love with her even though I told Zoey I'd love her forever."

A hand on his arm made him look up. "You can do both, you know. You can love Ashlinn and love Zoey."

He wanted to yank his arm away, but he didn't. "And how would that work, Cade? I feel like I'm cheating. Neither of them deserves a divided man."

"Neither?" He scoffed, shaking his head. "You speak as if Zoey is still here. She's gone, man. Sooner or later, you're going to have to accept it!"

"I don't want to accept it!" He did jerk his arm away then.

"And Ashlinn's complicated. I can't win. Maybe I'm supposed to be alone."

"Ashlinn's *health* is complicated. Mackenzie's talked to me about it. But it sure looks to me like that doesn't bother you."

"It doesn't. I've been around her enough to know how to help her."

"What's the problem, then?"

Ty's shoulders slumped. Fritz danced around his feet, and he picked him up. "She thinks she'd be a burden. And she thinks I'll never get over Zoey."

"I have to agree with her on the last point. I don't know what it's going to take for you to acknowledge that Zoey's not coming back. She's not suffering anymore. She's in heaven. And you're here. No matter how much you punish yourself by hiding out on this ranch or avoiding Ashlinn, that's not going to change."

"I didn't want to get over Zoey!"

"Too bad." Cade shifted his jaw. "That fearless kid who rode a sheep longer than anyone else at the rodeo is still in there somewhere, Ty. I suggest you find him, or life is going to pass you by."

Fearless? What a joke. He wasn't fearless. Probably never had been. What Cade didn't understand was that was exactly what he wanted—for life to pass him by. Get it over with. He didn't deserve to be happy.

Cade shook his head in annoyance. "I still think you should give a short speech to welcome everyone, but I have one prepared if you decide not to."

He hadn't prepared a speech, and he didn't see that changing. His phone dinged. He checked the text—it was from Ashlinn.

I don't want you to come over tomorrow. I'm not going to the fundraiser.

Disappointment stabbed his heart. She really was done with him. What had he expected? He hadn't reached out to her at all since Saturday. Should he even respond?

Okay.

As soon as he sent it, regrets crashed down. He wanted to wipe his hands down his cheeks and grind his teeth together and yell until he was out of breath. But he kept his emotions locked tight.

He didn't have a future with Ashlinn. The sooner he accepted it, the sooner he could resume his loner life on the ranch. Cade thought it was a punishment. It wasn't. It was the only way he knew how to survive.

Fritz licked his arm. *"He's alerting you."* He petted the dog. At least he wouldn't be completely alone. He had the best dog in the world. Too bad he couldn't have the best woman, too.

Chapter Thirteen

Thursday evening Ashlinn did something she hadn't done in a long time. She voluntarily called her mother. "Do you have time to talk, Mom?"

"Why? What's wrong?" Her mother sounded agitated, and Ashlinn could hear pots banging around in the background. "Are you having trouble keeping food down again?"

"No." Closing her eyes, she reached down from where she sat on the couch and petted Peanut. "I'm not calling about my health."

"Oh." The word lilted at the end. The sound of chopping filtered through. "What's going on?"

"Ty asked me to go with him to the fundraiser tomorrow night, and before you freak out, I told him no."

Chop, chop, chop.

"I'm glad you recognized your limits. I like Ty, but a crowded dinner would be too much for you."

Ashlinn thought of the room for the bridal party. How she could easily slip away with Peanut if he alerted her. She'd have time. She typically had a few minutes from the first alert. The room was quiet and comfortable, ideal for her to make it through an episode of low blood pressure.

"Did he ask you to be his date?" Her mother sounded curious.

"Yes." She hadn't thought she'd ever get close enough to a man to be turning down dates. The knowledge was bittersweet. "That's what I wanted to talk about."

The streaming of the faucet running made up for the silence. For once, her mother didn't have anything to say.

"Remember when we used to talk?" Ashlinn kept her tone light. "Back when I first went away to college? Every Sunday night, we had a standing phone date."

"I remember," she said softly. "I looked forward to your call all week."

"I want to get back to that."

"But we talk every day."

"No, I mean, I want to talk about things other than if I fainted, if my stomach is upset or how I slept."

"Like what?"

"Like you can tell me what's going on with work, or I can update you on the dogs Patrick is training."

Her mom sighed. "You want to pretend you don't have AAG."

The words were like a machete to her heart. She closed her eyes, trying to adjust to the pain. Her mother was determined to put her in a box labeled Sick and leave her there forever. A sarcastic reply hovered on the tip of her tongue, but she buried it.

Be patient with her.

"I don't want to pretend anything. I want my life to be more than my disease. Does it have to define every minute of my day?" Silence stretched. No chopping. No faucet running. "Mom?"

"I'm sorry. You're right." She let out a deep sigh. "I've been struggling lately. It's been hard having you move so far away."

"I know you worry, and I understand that it's hard."

"The house got so quiet after you left. I think it kind of hit me how stressful the past years have been. Last week I went to lunch with the new gal at work, and she said something that surprised me. She said I've been surviving on fear-fueled adrenaline all this time. I hadn't realized the toll it took on me. Don't get me wrong, your health improving was an answer to many prayers. I guess I worry that it won't last. That what you're going through is merely a good phase, and a bad one will be coming."

Ashlinn accepted the truth of her statement. "If it did, you'd be back in stress mode. Surviving on fear-fueled adrenaline again."

"I would do it in a heartbeat. I love you, Ashlinn. You know I love you. I hope you know I love you."

"Of course, Mom. I love you, too. I've always known that. You've been so good to me. I appreciate all the sacrifices you and Dad have made for me. I guess I want to be more to you than someone you worry about."

"I did my best, Ashlinn. I don't know what you want me to say."

"I know. I'm not trying to sound ungrateful. I guess I could use a shoulder to lean on. Someone to talk to."

"About what?"

"I told Ty I wasn't going to the fundraiser, and I also told him I can't spend time with him anymore."

"Why would you tell him that?"

The truth pained her. She didn't want to admit it, but she couldn't deny it any longer. "Because I love him. And you were right. He lost the woman he loved, and I won't put him through a lifetime with my health problems, even if he did feel the same about me. He doesn't. He's not over Zoey."

"A few days ago, I probably would have told you that you were being smart."

"And now?" Hope and fear battled.

"I don't know, Ashlinn. I saw how he was with you. He cares about you. Glances at you when you're not looking. Anticipates your needs before you do. How many times did he hand you your tumbler of water when we were together? I didn't want to admit it, but he's the kind of guy you can trust. Your dad and I already trust him from another state. I think he is over Zoey."

Could her mother be right? Ashlinn wasn't so sure. "I don't know what to do."

Her mom hesitated. "Pray."

"That's it?" She'd fully expected step-by-step instructions from her. She'd been getting them on most topics for years.

"Yes. Prayer is all you really need. Put it in God's hands, and He'll work it out for your good."

"I guess it can't hurt to try."

They talked for several more minutes, and Ashlinn promised she'd FaceTime her on Sunday night. They were reinstating their weekly call, this time with video. "I love you, Mom. Thanks for listening."

"I love you, too."

After the call ended, Ashlinn got to her feet with one destination in mind. The backyard. Her mom was right—she needed to pray. Ever since Ty had brought over the outdoor furniture, she'd taken to sitting there in the evenings—a nice change of pace from her living room or the training center.

"Come on, Peanut. Let's go outside."

She didn't have to tell him twice. The dog loved the backyard as much as she did. After grabbing her water and shoving the weighted blanket and blood pressure cuff into the tote, she and Peanut went out the back door. She kicked off her flip-flops. The grass was cool under her bare feet. She sat on one of the Adirondack chairs, placed the water on the table next to her, closed her eyes and let her folded hands rest on her stomach.

Lord, Mom made some good points. Ty is attentive and caring. But that doesn't mean he's ready for a relationship. I don't know if I am either. What if he gets tired of me fainting all the time? What if he resents me for not going to church with him or being able to get groceries on my own? God, I need You. I need discernment.

"Yoo-hoo!" A woman's voice startled her. Ashlinn's eyes opened, and her heartbeat pounded. Christy Moulten opened the fence gate and joined her in the backyard. "I hope it's okay for me to stop by."

"Of course." Ashlinn gestured to the chair next to her. "Have a seat."

"Thank you." Ty's mom took in the yard. "I love what you've done back here. Those lights add a festive touch."

"Ty brought them over and installed them for me."

"He did?" Christy, wearing jeans, sandals and a flowy top, settled into the other Adirondack chair. "I'm surprised."

"You are?" She shifted to see her better. "Why?"

"I didn't think he noticed things like that. He's been a bachelor for a long time."

Ashlinn didn't know how to respond, so she remained silent.

"Rumor has it you're not going to the fundraiser tomorrow."

"I'm not." Saying it brought a fresh batch of pain.

Christy nodded. "You know what's best for you. Char and Mackenzie and I can lend you a hand if you change your mind. We reserved a seat for you close to the hallway where the bridal room is located."

Her kindness took Ashlinn by surprise. "That's so thoughtful."

"It's the least I can do. I can't tell you how much of a difference you've made since arriving in Jewel River."

Ashlinn was taken aback. "Um, I think you have me mixed up with someone else."

Christy shook her head and laughed. "You're too modest. Patrick has told me all about how Bandit is well on his way to being a medical alert dog because of you. And all the help you gave Ty planning this fundraiser? It means a lot to everyone involved. He's not the most event-planner-type of person."

"I didn't do much."

Christy stretched her arm out to cover Ashlinn's hand. "You did. I've been mentally going through checklists of things Ty needed to take care of for the event, and I'm telling you it was hard not to ask for updates. But you helped him with all of it. Filled him in on the little things that easily slip through the cracks."

"He would have figured it out."

"Maybe. But you made it easy for him. And it's been a long time since I've seen my son leaving that ranch of his for anything other than filling up his gas tank, picking up groceries or going to church. I'm glad you've given him a reason to think of something other than cattle."

"I'm sure I haven't—"

"You have." Christy's expression was dead serious. "It takes a special person to do all that you're doing. I admire you. Life deals us with blows, and yours have been particularly harsh. You don't let them stop you. You're a strong woman, and my son would be blessed to have you in his life. I know I'm not supposed to say anything like that. You'll both tell me you're not dating or you're just friends or whatever fibs help you sleep at night. But I know. I know Ty. You're the one who helped get him out more, and I thank you for it. You're the one who brought his smile back." She pushed herself to stand. "And now I'll leave you. Please let me know if you change your mind about tomorrow night. I'd love to help you get ready, and we'll get you to the Winston."

Christy bent to give her a hug. Then she scratched behind Peanut's ears, waved goodbye and let herself out through the gate.

Ashlinn wasn't sure what had just happened, but the hope flooding her told her she had some thinking to do.

She'd blamed her mother for treating her like her disease defined her. But hadn't she been doing the same? Acting like she had little value? Assuming all she'd bring to a relationship was a lifetime of fainting spells and uncertainty?

Maybe she'd been cheating herself, too. What did she want out of life?

Closing her eyes, she could envision exactly what she wanted.

Ty. She wanted Ty. Rocking on his front porch with Peanut and Fritz. Days like these—helping Patrick at the training center—and more.

More than her current situation, too. She wanted to try new things. Go to church, even if she fainted. Attend one of Christy's book club meetings.

She wouldn't even mind going to the fundraiser—but she wasn't making that decision right now. And she didn't know if she could bear to see the look on Ty's face when he gave his speech. It would only remind her how much he loved Zoey, and how he'd never love Ashlinn as much.

Christy's words came back to her about being the one who brought back his smile.

Could she be wrong about the fundraiser? Lying to herself to protect her heart?

She'd see how she felt tomorrow. Then she'd decide if she could handle going or not. Her health was one thing—but her heart was another. She couldn't watch Ty mourn another woman. But then again, it might give her the closure she needed to survive life without him.

Ty stretched as high as he could for the box in his bedroom closet Thursday night. His fingertips shifted it a little. He was able to edge it forward enough to grasp it. Once he'd gotten it down, he stared at the cover for a few moments before padding out of the closet. The clock glowed 11:07 from the nightstand. Could he face the contents of the box?

He blew dust off the top, then sat on the bed and placed it next to him. Fritz danced around his feet, so he put him on the bed, too. After Fritz inspected the pillows, he came over and stuck his nose near the box, sniffing loudly.

"No, Fritz. These aren't treats." He caressed the dog's back, thankful for the distraction. He lifted the cover. Scattered photos and notes greeted him along with the memorial from Zoey's funeral.

God, I'm not ready for this. I should have chucked this box in the trash years ago.

He was finding it hard to swallow. He didn't want to face these memories. He should throw it away now. Better late than never.

"That fearless kid who rode a sheep..." Cade's voice ran through his head. *Fine.*

He selected a photo on top. One of those mini-Polaroids Zoey had loved. They'd smooshed their faces together. Her smile was wider than the big sky above. He brought it close to his eyes to study it. Man, she'd looked happy. And he had, too.

They'd both been young. The Ty staring back at him didn't have a wrinkle, and his current face showed the passage of time.

He placed the photo on the bed and selected a paper.

Didn't have to open it to know what it was. Zoey's first love note to him. They'd dated for a few months before he'd asked her to officially be his girlfriend. The following week, she'd handed him this note when he'd driven her to his ranch.

Opening it, he read it, and he frowned as he realized it didn't crush him the way he'd expected. Rather, it brought him back to a special time.

He went through every picture, every memento, until the box sat empty. Fritz had fallen asleep. Ty had expected hot, scalding tears at the pain of missing her. But they hadn't come.

After placing everything back in the box, he set it on the dresser and reclined on the bed with his back resting against the pillows. For years, Ty had pictured Zoey here in his house. She'd been here many times before she'd passed away.

But there was only one woman he could picture here now.

Ashlinn. Her long blond hair and big blue eyes, her radiant face. A golden retriever who helped keep her safe.

Ty wanted to help keep her safe, too. He wanted to hear about her day and listen to her advice. He enjoyed her companionship.

She'd made him like himself again.

Swinging his legs over the side of the bed, he picked out several photos from the box and walked them to the kitchen counter. Then he found a notepad and pen, and returned to the bed where Fritz snored. And he wrote out exactly what he wanted to tell everyone who came to the fundraiser.

When he finished, he read through it, scratching out words and adding new ones in the margins.

Dare he go through with this? Could he really admit everything he'd written? To the entire town?

Yeah. He wanted fearless Ty back. And this would be a good place to start.

Chapter Fourteen

Ty checked his appearance in the full-length mirror of the bridal room at the Winston. He'd decided to wear a suit. After all, this shindig had been his idea. He adjusted his tie, shook out his sleeves and got closer to the mirror to make sure he hadn't missed any spots shaving. Guests would be arriving soon, and Erica had told him he could use this room to practice his speech. He'd practiced it twice, and both times he'd barely gotten through it. He'd had to cough and clear his throat. He doubted he'd make it through the entire thing tonight.

Fearless? Yeah, right.

For the past hour, his mom and Charlene had been fussing about the placement of the auction items. Thankfully, Cade was out there smoothing things over. The aroma of barbecue and smoked chicken filled the air, and every now and then, he'd hear, "Check. Check. Hot mic."

The staff they'd hired had been setting the programs on each table when he'd slipped away to this room. He only had a few minutes before he'd be forced to do the unthinkable—greet everyone and give a speech in front of a hundred and fifty people.

Fritz let out a yip near his feet. Ty had talked to his mom and Patrick, and they'd urged him to bring Fritz and tell everyone how he'd helped a veteran. Mackenzie had agreed to keep the dog with her while Ty was giving his speech.

"Hey, there, buddy." Ty bent to pick up the dog. "You look pretty good in that vest. I guess we're both as ready as can be expected, huh?"

"Yip!"

"Right back atcha." Ty ruffled the fur on his neck.

The door opened, and Cade, Mackenzie, Charlene and his mom entered the room.

"How are you feeling, Ty?" Mom came over and straightened his lapel.

"Good," he said. "A little nervous." Okay, a lot nervous.

"I would be, too." Charlene patted his arm. "You clean up good, cowboy."

"Thanks, Char." He nodded to her. She'd been his mom's best friend for as long as he could remember and had been like a second mom to him all these years. If he was being vulnerable, he might as well go all the way. He kissed her cheek. "Thanks for always being there for me."

"Oh, you!" She blushed, swatting her hand at the air.

"You did a good job with the table for Zoey." His mom studied him. "You sure you're okay?"

"I'm okay." His cheeks puffed as he blew out a breath.

"Want me to give the speech?" Cade asked. He had a sheepish air about him.

"No. I'm giving it. You were right." Ty stood taller. "About that and the other stuff, too."

To his shock, Cade put his arms around him and gave him a full hug. "I'm proud of you."

His chest swelled at all their support. He'd taken it for granted for a long time. Not anymore.

Mackenzie stepped forward. "Why don't I take Fritz so

you can greet people as they come in? Unless you'd prefer Christy greet them."

"No, I'll greet people." He met Cade's eyes. His brother mouthed, "Fearless."

For some reason that made him smile.

"Thank you—all of you." These were his people. They'd stuck by him, pushed him when he'd needed pushing and let him figure out his own path after Zoey died. "I haven't been easy to deal with for many years. I don't know if I ever will be, but I appreciate you all sticking by me. And I really appreciate all the help with this event. Now, I'd better get out there."

"We love you. We're proud of you. You're going to be great!" Mom clapped, and her eyes were suspiciously damp.

"Come on." Cade gestured to the door. "It's go time."

They all chattered as they left the room. Ty was the last to leave. But first, he paused to pray. *God, I need Your help tonight. Help me be fearless.*

And with that, he strode out the door with his head held high.

Tonight, he'd honor Zoey. Help Patrick's training center. And before the night was over, he was going to tell Ashlinn exactly what she meant to him.

He needed her. He loved her. And he wasn't letting anything stand in his way any longer.

Ashlinn peeked over at Clem as he drove her to the Winston. He gave her a sideways glance and a slight nod. "Your dog okay back there?"

She checked over her shoulder. Peanut sat in the middle of the backseat, and his panting smile assured her he was fine.

"He's great. He actually loves riding in vehicles."

Clem grunted.

Her nerves were wound tighter than a ball of yarn, and riding to the fundraiser with Clem wasn't helping them. When she'd called Christy an hour ago, she'd thought maybe Mackenzie or Cade would drive her. But they'd all headed to the Winston early to help set up. So... Clem had volunteered. He'd picked her up in his late-model truck, which, admittedly, was a smooth ride.

"You about to faint? Is that why your hands are fidgeting?"

She hadn't realized she was wringing her hands. She pressed them flat on her lap. "No. I'm a little nervous."

"About what?" He kept his eyes on the road ahead.

How was she supposed to answer that? About possibly fainting in front of the entire town? Or witnessing Ty mourn the love of his life? A toss-up.

"I haven't been out in public like this since before my diagnosis."

"I'm not surprised." He grunted. Then he glanced at her and appeared to be genuinely curious. "What causes your problems? Christy said something about A&P or AARP, I can't remember."

She suppressed a snort. No, a grocery store or a membership to the senior citizen organization wasn't causing her problems. "I have AAG. It's an autoimmune disease that attacks my autonomic nervous system."

"Give it to me in English, girlie," he said sternly.

"The things we take for granted—our heart beating, how we digest food—my body doesn't handle them correctly."

"The dog back there helps?"

"He does. I mean, he can't do much when I have stomach problems, but he knows when my blood pressure dips, and his alerts give me time to get to a safe position before I faint."

"And you faint a lot?" He didn't sound as gruff. "How often? Once an hour? Twice?"

She almost laughed, but then reality hit her. At one point, she had fainted that often and more.

"Sometimes only a few times each day."

"So two or three times a day?" His gray eyes widened as he shot her a look.

"Yeah, it's much better now. I used to faint almost every time I stood. I was basically bedridden for years. The doctors wanted me to try a plasma treatment, and it helped me. Then I got Peanut. Life is much better now."

She admired the beauty of Wyoming for a few miles, thankful for the silence.

"You sure you want to go to this dinner?" he asked.

"I'm sure."

"The food will be good—Drake Arless knows how to smoke meat—but I've got to warn you, the ladies are going to descend on you like a flock of starving ravens in the dead of winter."

She scrunched her nose, confused. "What do you mean?"

"You're single. And you have a dog. They'll have you married off to one of the locals in no time."

"I'm not sure how Peanut factors into it." She started to feel lightheaded at the thought of all that attention even if Clem was dead wrong.

"A golden retriever? Pshaw." He shook his head. "The cowboys around here would date you just for the dog, but you're pretty, too."

She relaxed a bit at the compliment.

"If you need me to carry you in, say the word. I still rope calves, and these old shoulders can haul a heavy load."

"Um, thank you, but that won't be necessary." She would

tuck away the offer to examine later. Did he think he'd haul her into the Winston like a side of beef?

"Fine, but the offer stands. Although, you'd be better off with Ty carrying you. He's a good man. A fine cowboy. Quiet. That's a point in his favor. You could do a lot worse than settling down with a man who keeps to himself like Ty."

Where had that come from? This conversation was zig-zagging out of control.

"Of course, he probably still thinks he's in love with that brown-haired girl he'd been ready to marry. We all felt bad when she died. If you ask me, he needs to pull up his britches and move on. When I saw you two at that ridiculous Shakespeare movie—I hope to never sit through one of those again—I was glad. Figured you two would make a good couple. But he's been hiding away again, and I don't like it."

"I don't like it either," she said softly.

He nodded in agreement. "Well, here we are. Don't go getting out of the seat until I open the door for you. Christy would beat me over the head with a wooden spoon if you hurt yourself before I get you inside." Clem parked the truck and got out.

She giggled, which turned into laughing, and she couldn't stop. Maybe she was growing hysterical. The past twenty-four hours had been odd, to say the least.

Clem took her tote and let Peanut out of the backseat, and she'd gotten herself under control by the time he opened her door. When he offered her his hand, she accepted, and he helped her down with a gentleness she'd never thought possible. She took hold of the handle of Peanut's harness. Then Clem held out his arm, and she took it, too.

"Ready?" he asked.

"Ready. Can we go in through the side door? That way I can set up a station in the bridal room in case I faint."

"A station? What are we talking about?"

She explained about the weighted blanket as they crossed the lot to the side door. Getting through the dinner would probably be the easy part. The difficulty would be in figuring out how to pull Ty aside. She had to tell him how she really felt about him.

She loved him. And she was ready to take a chance on love. She just hoped tonight didn't prove what he'd been telling her all along—that he preferred a dead woman to her.

Chapter Fifteen

"Thank you all for coming." Ty had spent almost thirty minutes shaking hands and accepting hugs from the members of the community who'd come out tonight. He'd noticed a common theme. They all thanked him for putting on the event, raved about how the service dog training center was a wonderful cause, and then they'd shared a personal story about Zoey.

How she'd babysat their kids when she was in high school, or the time she'd messed up her piece at the piano recital and gave a little curtsy that everyone thought was the cutest thing ever. Throughout the process, Ty realized she hadn't only mattered to him. She'd touched many people's lives. And they all spoke of her fondly.

No one had forgotten her.

He wouldn't either.

As everyone got settled at their tables and turned their attention to him, he smoothed out the paper where he'd written his speech. He took a moment to get his nerves settled.

"When I first had the idea of doing something to honor Zoey's memory, I didn't dare dream this many people would respond. You have other things to do on a Friday night, and I appreciate you joining me here. First, special thanks to Erica and Dalton Cambridge for supplying the Winston free of charge."

Everyone applauded. Ty studied the crowd until he found Erica and Dalton sitting a few tables back. He nodded to them. Erica clasped her hands over her heart as she beamed.

"Thank you to my family and everyone who volunteered to put this on. As most of you know, Zoey and I were engaged, but God had other plans for her." Could he say the next part out loud? "Most of you haven't seen me much since she passed. I've struggled with grief. Life lost its color. When Patrick Howard moved to town and opened Howard Service Dogs, my dear mother—" he pointed to her table "—told me all about the work he was doing to help people with illnesses and other problems affecting their daily lives. Mom mentioned him needing volunteers. I ignored her."

Titters of laughter circled the room.

"Once again, God had other plans. See Mackenzie over there?" He pointed to her and Cade. Fritz sat on her lap. "She's holding Fritz, a miniature dachshund who used to be a therapy dog for a veteran. When his owner passed, Fritz came to live with me. I didn't know I needed him. I do. He recognizes when I'm feeling down and comforts me."

At the table in front of him, Clem slipped into the chair next to his mother, and to her left, Charlene was dabbing at her eyes with a tissue. "One of Jewel River's newest residents, Ashlinn Burnier, is helping Patrick train dogs to detect medical issues. Ashlinn's medical alert dog, Peanut, allows her to live independently. Training the dogs, housing them, and helping clients learn how to work with their dogs takes money. Every penny we raise tonight will go to Howard Service Dogs."

He could end the speech there. But he was ready to be that fearless kid again.

"Ashlinn helped me plan this event. I couldn't have done it without her. She isn't here, and I wish she was. I'd tell her thank you. Thank you for getting me out of my rut. Thank you for generously giving your time to an event honoring a woman I loved long ago. Thank you for allowing me to see life through a lens of gratitude, rather than one of self-pity."

He glanced at his mom, and her eyes shined brightly as she nodded.

"I'd tell Ashlinn a few other things, too. I'd tell her that Zoey was a beautiful woman inside and out, and I've been ready to let her go for a while. Yes, I've been fighting it, but I'm ready. I'll always have good memories of her. And I'm ready to make new memories. With another woman who is beautiful inside and out. I fell in love with Ashlinn Burnier, and I'm going to hand the mic to my brother so I can drive to her house and tell her myself."

The crowd rose to their feet, clapping, whooping and whistling.

Ty set the microphone in the stand and strode away from the podium. His chest felt tight to bursting in the best possible way.

He was going to win Ashlinn back no matter what it took. Tonight.

Ashlinn had been holding Peanut's harness in the doorway of the bridal room as Ty gave his speech. As soon as she heard, "I've been ready to let her go for a while," she hurried down the hall and emerged into the main area. Her gaze landed on Ty as he jogged in the opposite direction.

What if he left before she could catch him?

With everyone on their feet whooping and hollering, she had no shot at catching his attention. Her heart pounded, her pulse raced, and Peanut licked her hand. She ignored the dog to move forward through the crush of people. But Peanut blocked her path.

Tears pressed against her eyes. Not now. Not when she had a million things to say to Ty.

"Quiet everyone." Clem's stern voice filled the room. Ashlinn jerked her attention to the podium. The room went silent. "Ty Moulten, get your buns back in here."

Ashlinn had no idea if Ty obeyed or not. Peanut continued to block her path. Either she retreated to the bridal room now, or she'd pass out here.

"Ashlinn's here. Her dog is, too. You made a smart choice with that woman, Ty. Who cares if she faints now and then? Could be worse. We all remember when Walt, may he rest in peace, coughed up blood at church or when Betty Jane had flatulence through no fault of her own—"

Christy grabbed the mic from him. "No need to go down memory lane, Clem. Ty, hon, Ashlinn's over there." She pointed the mic to Ashlinn. "Now, who's ready to eat? It's past time we dug into this delicious barbecue. I'm starving."

Clem and Christy to the rescue. Another round of applause went up, and Ashlinn, lightheaded, made her way back to the bridal room. Peanut licked her hand and blocked her path again before she got inside. She didn't know if she should laugh or cry. She'd finally gotten the courage to come here, and her body was threatening to thwart her plans.

A strong arm curved below her knees, and Ty swept her into his arms, carried her into the room and kicked the door closed behind him. She leaned her cheek against his shoulder.

Her strong cowboy.

He sat on the couch with her on his lap. She turned to look at him. She'd never seen him so intense. His brown eyes gleamed with appreciation for her.

"You came," he said.

"I did."

"You look…" his gaze took her in from head to toe "…absolutely stunning. This dress—" he shook his head, awe in his expression "—wow."

"This old thing?" The pale aqua dress had been sitting in her closet for years, never worn. "You did good up there, Ty."

Peanut sat on the floor next to them, rested his chin on the couch and stared at her. She petted his head. Ty handed her the tumbler of water. She took a drink.

"Do you need to get on the floor?" He caressed her bare arm.

"The only place I need to be is right here in your arms."

He searched her eyes, then turned his attention to her lips. Taking his sweet time, he lowered his mouth to hers. The kiss started out slow, tender. Then it grew insistent. She kissed him back, wanting him to know how much he meant to her. How his speech—in front of all of Jewel River, no less—had made her feel like the most loved woman on earth.

Peanut jumped on the couch and set his paws on her lower legs. Ashlinn's arms were wrapped around Ty's neck, and she dragged one down to pet the big guy. "Good boy."

"Let's get you on the floor." He helped her down and sat next to her, keeping his arm around her shoulders.

"You meant everything you said, didn't you?"

"I did. Every word."

"I have things to say to you, too. I might mangle this or faint during it, but please hear me out."

"You don't have to—"

"Oh, but I do. You make me feel normal. When I'm with you, I'm not merely an invalid. I'm your friend who happens to pass out a lot. Did you know your mom stopped by last night?" His muscles tensed, and she patted his chest. "Don't worry. She told me something I needed to hear."

"What did she say?"

"She told me that I'm making a difference in people's lives, and that I'm strong."

"You do make a difference, and you are strong."

"I have a hard time seeing it." Her heart no longer pounded, and her pulse had slowed. Peanut wandered around the room. "All I could see was my limitations. But here's the thing. I called my mother. We had a good talk. I explained how I wanted us to have actual conversations. She admitted it's been difficult to return to normal life after the stress of the previous years."

"Makes sense."

"Afterward, it kind of hit me that in some ways I do the same thing as she does. I don't always see myself beyond my illness. I let it stop me from doing things I want to do."

"You have a good reason." With the softest touch, he stroked her hair.

"Maybe before Peanut, I did. But I'm ready to expand my horizons. I'd like to go to church with you."

"You mean it?" A smile spread across his face.

"And I think I could go to the grocery store."

"There wouldn't be a place for you to sit if you fainted." His forehead creased in worry.

"I've thought of that. What if I used a wheelchair?"

"Yes. Then you wouldn't get injured if you did pass out." He kissed her forehead. "What else do you want to do?"

She twined her fingers in his. "I want to go back to your ranch and rock on your front porch. Watch the world go by."

"It's my favorite place to be." He brought their joined hands to his lips, kissing her knuckles. "I love you, Ashlinn. I want you to know I *am* over Zoey. I talked to her parents, went through old photos and letters, and I wasn't devastated. I've been holding on to guilt over her death for years.

Afraid to move past it. Afraid I'll forget her. Afraid to try again and lose again."

"Are you still afraid?" She stilled, not quite trusting he could handle being with her.

"I'll always be afraid of losing you. I think that's part of love. The highs and the lows. But I'm not letting it stop me. I don't want to miss out on another minute with you. I love you, Ashlinn, and I'm bound and determined to be a man worthy of you."

"Oh, Ty!" She was getting emotional and didn't care. "You're worthy. Don't ever think you're not worthy. If I get to be too much for you—"

"Never. Don't even say it."

"But I have to. My health could get worse. I could be bed-ridden again."

"My love isn't conditional on your health. I love you now. I'll love you through anything. You're the one for me."

"And you're the one for me."

Chapter Sixteen

"Can we come in?"

Half an hour had passed since Ty had brought Ashlinn to the couch. He stared into her pretty blue eyes, and she nodded.

"Come in," he yelled.

The door to the bridal room opened, and Fritz raced to them. After helping Ashlinn to her feet, Ty picked up the dog and slid his arm around her waist. Cade, Mackenzie, Patrick, Mom, Clem and Charlene piled into the room.

"So?" His mother clearly couldn't take the suspense. She looked like a balloon ready to pop. Fritz wiggled, and Ty set him on the floor. He immediately trotted to Peanut.

Ty pressed Ashlinn closer to his side. "I love her."

"And I love him." She bit her lower lip, glancing up at him.

"Shouldn't you be on that rug, girlie?" Clem gave a pointed stare to her, then to the rug where they'd put her folded weighted blanket.

"I'm not going to faint. Not at the moment, anyhow."

"Right. That dog of yours isn't licking your hand." The man rubbed his chin. "Proceed."

Cade surged forward to clap Ty on the back, and Mackenzie drew Ashlinn into a big hug. Then Mom hugged her and Charlene. The women were talking a mile a minute, and he didn't even attempt to decipher what they were saying.

"Fearless," Cade said. "That speech. Whew. People will be talking about that one for years."

"We might not even discuss the book this month at book club. We'll rehash your speech instead. You made me tear up." Mom came in for a hug. "I didn't know you could be so romantic."

"I see you came to your senses." Clem hooked his thumbs in his belt loops and rocked back on his heels. "I expect to see more of you around town."

"I don't know about that." Ty grimaced. "I'm not a social butterfly."

"Is she?" Clem hitched his head to Ashlinn.

"Not really," she said. "A quiet, simple life is what I want."

"Well, there you go."

His mom turned to Ashlinn. "Now will you come to book club?"

Ashlinn met Ty's gaze. He shrugged.

"I'll think about it."

"Good." His mother took Ashlinn's hands in hers and squeezed. "We'd love to have you. And like I said, no one will care if you faint. Mary fell asleep with a cookie in her hand last month. She startled and that cookie went flying."

"Christy." Clem sidled next to her.

"Yes?" She turned to him with an expectant expression.

"What do you think?"

"About what?"

"About making it official."

"I told you I'm not getting married." She huffed.

"No one said a thing about marriage, woman. I'm talking about dating. You and me. I know I'm old and mean. And you're spry and beautiful and fun. You make me feel alive."

"You think I'm fun?" His mom blinked in surprise. "But all I do is yell at you."

"Pshaw." He waved in dismissal. "I need a little yelling at me."

Ty met Cade's gaze—as confused and stricken as his own surely was.

"Then, yes, Clem. I'll be your girlfriend. If that's what you're asking."

"That's what I'm asking. Didn't you hear a word I said? Cheese and biscuits."

"I heard you! See? This is what I was talking about last week. You miss social cues and come across as rude. You are the most exasperating man."

Clem took her hand and tugged her close. "And you're cute when you're upset."

"I am?"

Cade threw his hands in the air. "Okay, what is going on?"

"Well, honey, Clem and I have been getting close—"

"Understood." Cade held up a palm. "I can handle you two dating—at least I think I can—but I draw the line at you two kissing. Take it somewhere else."

Mom gave the biggest eye roll Ty had ever seen, and Clem scoffed. "We're old. We ain't dead."

"I'd rather be dead than watch you kiss my mother." Cade took a step closer to Clem. The older man narrowed his eyes, standing steady and tall. The room had grown quiet, and everyone watched them through wide eyes.

Then Clem smiled—Ty wasn't sure he'd ever seen the man smile—and gave Cade a nod. "That's why I like you, Cade. Your brother, too. You don't shy away from speaking your mind."

"We all know you never shy away from it either." Their mother elbowed Clem's side. "Let's get back to the dinner." She turned to Ashlinn. "You're probably starving. Want us to bring some food back here for you?"

"No, thanks." Ashlinn beamed at Ty. "I'd like to eat out there with Ty."

"You're sure?" He didn't want her to feel embarrassed or push herself too hard. "People are going to come over to meet you. They might have a lot of questions."

"I hope they do. It's time I met my neighbors. I have a feeling I'm going to be living in Jewel River for a long time."

Ty pulled her into his arms and hugged her tightly, then whispered near her ear. "If I have anything to say about it, you'll be living here forever."

Epilogue

The last time Ty had attended one of these meetings, he'd been a different person—a man afraid of interacting with people around town. He still enjoyed the solitude of riding horseback around his ranch. Still preferred being home to going out. But he no longer avoided people.

Ashlinn brought out the best in him.

He glanced at her and gave her hand a squeeze. Three months had passed since the fundraiser, and she still made his heart do cartwheels. With the money the dinner had raised and Cade and Mackenzie's matching donation, Patrick had been able to purchase the van he'd wanted. He'd already used it a few times to bring clients to the center and teach them how to handle their dogs.

Ashlinn still loved working there. A new dog had arrived last week that showed promise as a medical alert dog. Ty sure was proud of her. With Christmas only two weeks away, the weather was too cold for her to walk to work. Patrick or Mackenzie picked her up and dropped her off on the days she felt up to it. Her health remained about the same as when she'd arrived in the summer.

"Oh, Erica?" Angela Zane waved her hand frantically. Erica Cambridge stood at the podium. Ty might be mistaken, but was she pretending not to see the waving hand? "Erica!"

"Yes, Angela." Erica turned to the woman.

"Joey asked me to announce that he won't be making the Shakespeare film this year. He was accepted into a fancy film school in Boston. We're so proud of him. But I have to admit, I'm sad our Shakespeare-in-the-Park films will be ending."

"Good for Joey!" Erica beamed. "We're very proud of him. We'll miss his movies, too. They've become a tradition."

"I know. That's what I told him." Angela wore the face of a proud grandma. "He wanted to share a little something tonight. Can you get the audio-visual equipment ready?"

Erica's gaze found Dalton, and she struck the air with her index finger. He nodded, pulling down the screen, while Cade went over to the light switches on the wall.

"What's going on?" Ashlinn whispered. Peanut sat by her side.

"I'm not sure. I'm guessing Joey made a video."

A few minutes later, Cade cut the lights, and the video began with flames burning in the center and expanding outward. A low male voice began to narrate.

"Joseph Zane would like to thank the Jewel River Legacy Club for giving him an outlet to use his digital graphics skills." A plunger detonated dynamite, and explosives roared, blowing up the screen. "If not for the Shakespeare-in-the-Park movies, he wouldn't have gotten accepted into Boston University's VFX, Animation and Interactive Media program. Don't worry. He won't forget where he came from. Jewel River will always be home."

The film cut to Joey typing at a computer and waving to the camera. A rocket flew across the screen, leaving words written from the exhaust. *This isn't the end. It's the beginning.*

Cade turned on the lights, and everyone got to their feet

and clapped. When the applause died down, Angela was wiping tears as she smiled.

"We're so proud of him and all he's done for our community, Angela," Erica said. "Tell him he's welcome to put on another film anytime. He's blessed us with his talents."

The phrase stuck with Ty as the meeting continued. *He's blessed us with his talents.*

When the meeting ended, Ty stood. "Just a minute, everyone. I have an announcement."

The members turned to him with curious expressions.

"Over the weekend, I asked this beautiful woman to marry me. To my relief, Ashlinn Burnier said yes."

Cheers rose. People came over to congratulate them. Mary, his mother and Angela surrounded Ashlinn for several minutes. He was proud that she'd gotten the courage to get out more. Sure, she'd passed out at church twice. No one batted an eye when she and Peanut came into stores. They all liked her. How could anyone not like Ashlinn?

Soon everyone trickled out. He and Ashlinn, Clem and his mom, and Cade and Mackenzie left together. Out in the parking lot, Cade and Mackenzie said goodbye to them. Clem took his mother's hand, and they walked ahead, chatting, then arguing. Ty put his arm around Ashlinn's shoulders. The dark sky was full of twinkling stars. Snowflakes began to fall.

"That went better than I expected," Ty said.

"I'm so happy for Joey."

"Me, too." He squeezed her shoulder. "And I'm happy for us. What Angela said back there, 'He blessed us with his talents.' I feel the same about you. You bless us with your talents, Ash. You're patient and kind and the best person I know."

"See? This is why I love you. You only see the good in me. Never the bad."

He kissed her temple. "You're all good. Through and through."

"I'm not, and you know it. You, on the other hand, are about as perfect a cowboy as has ever lived."

"Me?" He pretended to be surprised. "I know better, but you keep thinking that."

"Are we going back to my place to watch the Christmas movie I recorded?"

"Yes."

"What about going with me to your mother's book club in January?"

"I draw the line there."

"I don't blame you." She nestled into his side. "You're still my cowboy."

"I'll forever be your cowboy."

* * * * *

If you enjoyed this K-9 Companions book, be sure to look for The Soldier's K-9 Companion *by Belle Calhoune, available in August 2025, wherever Love Inspired books are sold.*

And don't miss a new Wyoming-set miniseries from Jill Kemerer, coming soon!

Dear Reader,

Ty and Ashlinn spent six years struggling with problems I hope most people never experience. Losing the woman he loved devastated Ty. And Ashlinn's future was permanently changed by a debilitating disease. Peanut helped her reclaim some independence, and when Ty adopted Fritz, he got the comforting companion he hadn't known he needed. Dogs help us in many ways—emotionally, physically—and with their unconditional love.

Ty and Ashlinn had spiritual hurdles to overcome, too. Ty finally let go of survivor's guilt and embraced letting people into his life. And Ashlinn was able to see herself as more than an invalid with help from the Bible and her new friends.

I pray you embrace God's blessings, too, no matter how difficult your circumstances may be. He loves you, and He'll never let you go.

I hope you enjoyed this book in the Wyoming Legacies series. I love connecting with readers. Feel free to email me at jill@jillkemerer.com or write me at P.O. Box 2802, White-house, Ohio, 43571.

Blessings to you!
Jill Kemerer